Heel!

Heel!

THE NEW WORLD ORDER

MADAME DE MORVILLE

STILETTO BOOKS

Published by Stiletto Books in 2002

© Stiletto Books 2001

First published in Great Britain in 2002 by Stiletto Books
An imprint of Dilston Press Limited, Hilmarton, Calne, SN11 8RZ, England

Dilston Press Limited Reg. No. 3411422

A CIP catalogue record for this book is available
from the British Library

ISBN 1 903908 05 1

Cover photograph by Nic Marchant

Book designed and typeset by Andrew Burrell

Printed and bound in Great Britain by
Butler & Tanner Ltd, Somerset

Internet website: www.stilettobooks.com

Heel! *is a state of mind, the politics of the mundane divine, a polished stiletto boot, bloodless revolution, the new world order.*

MADAME DE MORVILLE

Contents

Foreword

Do you, the male reader, wake from your dreams with an aching skull, as if the skin and bone of your forehead have been further inclined by its repeated impact against the taut leather stretched between the smooth thighs of the well polished and chaste skirt? Do your arms, withdrawn and bound behind your inclined back, reflexively return to their position of prayer after their release by the patient and resisting Mistress? Do you, while kneeling with eyes closed, dimly perceive the surface shine of a polished pyramid built apparently from black granite or rubber, that has been inserted in your sleep deep within your now malleable cranium? Do you feel drawn to enter into this pyramid shape and then to travel within it as if within a space-ship into those dark worlds ruled over by the black devas? Do you, the feminine reader and Mistress, when you are seated in the darkness alone, begin to sense through the animated leather of your pointed shoe or boot, through its curving stiletto heel, the faint touch of a man's invisible tongue? Then you are ready, if not yet prepared, to benefit from the nocturnal experiences written down by this pioneering man who has ventured in full consciousness into the parallel life of Heel!, the organisation that has its origins in the heavenly constellation of Bootes.

It has been requested of me by the male and english employees of our imprint, Stiletto Books, that this book should appear under

===

my name since the author of the twenty journal entries selected for publication as a book, has regrettably and indefinitely been detained in the otherworldy version of your Venice which is known to us as the Republic of Venetia - some accident on a trampoline in a Venetian palazzo that he was visiting as a nocturnal tourist, whereby he was seen to vanish through a point in the *trompe l'oeil* ceiling, held in the jaws and serrated forelegs of a giant scarab-beetle ridden by a rubber-clad lady. She, being the owner of at least one version of the palace, was observed dangling a lengthy bull-whip as though it were a wriggling type of fishing-line, above his rubber-encased and quite anonymous head.

Your Earth will shortly be merged with the etheric version of your planet which is governed from the Republic of Venetia by the Council of Ten, the five masked members of which, being the feminine representatives of the Goddess, meet annually on the night of the carnival in what is called by you, the Doge's Palace. The time of transformation, of celebration for you, the Mistress, and of eternal servitude for you, the male reader, the securely bound rubber-man [the internal organs of whom are to be converted to run on a liquid form of the same material], is imminent; an interval of time has been entered during which your dying planet, together with the Goddess-defying scientist and the overly virile and destructive seed of the patriarch, are each to be handed over, to fall into the leather- or rubber-gloved hands of the whip-wielding and vengeful membership of Heel!, the men to be then tried and sentenced in the Hall of Judgement in the Temple of Queen Hatshepsut in Egypt's Valley of the Queens. There is no other exit that remains open to you, except that of becoming a whip-woman [the member of Heel!], a rubber-man adapted to the new conditions [the tran-

substantiated slave], or being subjected to reptilian metamorpho-
sis for violations of Divine Law [the fate in store for the male,
white-coated geneticist, the environmental terrorist]. To derive the
fullest benefit from this book so that you can most easily achieve
this transition between alternate realities, the transfiguration required of you, I request that each of you reads in addition to this
slave's journal those texts of mine that I have instructed Stiletto
Books to include within the Select Bibliography.

MADAME DE MORVILLE

Introduction

Despite the assurances given by Madame de Morville in the fore-
word to this book, that the devoted reader and potential rubberman
will not be excluded from the new world order of Heel!, we at
Stiletto Books nevertheless feel that some more intimate evidence
of the nature of the personal transition and conversion involved
should be furnished to calm the nerves of men such as your selves
who may through fear remain indoors and alone while the regular
world outside slowly or more abruptly is substituted by that of the
other world of Heel!.

   With permission therefore from the Paris offices of Heel! magazine, from Madame de Morville on her return from her chateau in
the south-west of France, we have printed the following extracts
from the journal of a common man, typical in his outlook and de-
meanour of the average city-dweller of today, and in the basic
language employed by him to record his experiences and nocturnal disappearances. We, ourselves, who are subject to the very same
devastation of personality and physique, have found comfort in
such mundane descriptions forwarded to our London offices from
Paris for printing in future issues of Heel! magazine.

STILETTO BOOKS

Heel!

ONE

The Scarab-Beetle

JANUARY 15TH

Last night I woke fully within a dream, in a city I recognized as
New York. The streets were flooded with a black viscous liquid,
the familiar buildings substituted by the facades of polished black
obelisks. Rays of cosmic light were absorbed, re-emitted, by the
black granite surfaces of a central pyramid. Through their light,
flying out of the blackness of this otherworldly scene, I saw scarab-
beetles of huge size, some ridden in formation by whip-wielding
women. I myself was gripped about my masculine torso by the
front, serrated legs of one such predatory beetle, being shown in
this irregular fashion the sights of both an alien and unforgiving
cityscape. At equal intervals, my body was held out from beneath
the beetle's exoskeletal undercarriage so that the rubber-clad rider
might inspect the night's catch for signs of life, of my adaptability
to the atmosphere of her version of New York, to her perverted
world. With my neck thrown back, as if attempting a somersault
to freedom, but caught instead frozen beneath her heavenly gaze, I
observed while being dangled there in mid-air, the points of her

polished boots extending beyond, in front of the beetle's skull. Positioned between them, poised above a narrow-waisted, full-breasted figure which was concealed behind a coating of rubber material, her finely-boned face, mesmerizing by its beauty, stared down beneath heavy lids, exotic eyebrows and Egyptian head-dress. Responding to some signal given perhaps by the depressive tapping of stiletto on the echoing chamber of the beetle's unquestioning brain, as if I too were to be brainwashed the better to accept this undemocratic culture, I was as suddenly released from the imprisoning grip, plummeting past the horizontally slit windows that showed the smooth obelisks to be populated by identically dressed and heeled women, down into the environing sea of black rubber. I awoke short of breath, coughing a dark liquid, half-suffocated by my immersion in that other New York, but alive.

I washed my face more thoroughly than is usual, having first confirmed that the world outside my dream, that lay beyond and was framed by my rectangular balcony window, was indeed as it should be, rubberless and without any infestation of marauding beetles. My towel would – my brain now in overdrive – require not just a regular wash producing grey-black suds of frothing water to be flushed away with the events of last night, but its burning and the returning of its elements to the ether, to the otherworldly Egyptian-looking women who perhaps still lurked on the backs of scarab-beetles surveying the commuting men below with predatory intent. There was in me when the moment came for the match to be lit in the space made beside my plastic dinner-table with its solitary chair [now withdrawn from the balcony so as not to appear inviting to the alien woman], a certain reluctance to destroy with fire the rubbery material covering my towel. Some portion of my waking persona had during my nocturnal adventuring caught the bug of the fetishist's perversion of which I intended resolutely to be rid, the putting on of my city suit, the resulting confidence in the prevailing routine, falsely convincing me – this note being added later to the journal entry above – of the ease with which this sick brand of mental illness can be thrown off by positive thought and the healthy affirmation of what seemed before to be important and democratically right. I resolved however, on the morning of January 27th, wiping my curling lip finally free of the same black material [which were it alive, might have been supposed to be in possession of its own intent to spread its dark appeal and gleaming madness], to make no mention of this experience to my office colleagues, unless some change in my own appearance prompted their intrusive questioning.

TWO

The Fountain of Evening

JANUARY 27TH

I have the feeling of being rolled from side to side, back and forth across my bed . . . of my dreaming body becoming by this process detached from the physical. Sensation of being rolled beneath the pointed feminine sole of a shoe or boot, backwards and forwards to the cliff's edge, until the cool leather launches me with a violent thrust into the abyss below. Falling into blackness, through a seemingly fathomless intervening space which grows more resistant to my descent, more viscous, before my re-emergence in rubbery form, I am grabbed again by the indigenous scarab-beetle, pulled clear of the street and lifted far up amongst the skyscraping obelisks. The beetle's legs are extended forwards to reveal the hardening new skin of my transforming body to the stiletto-heeled and whip-wielding rider. I am by this brief inspection again rejected, dropped down past the gradually sloping walls of smooth granite, to whose hieroglyphic imprints armoured and unearthly iguanas cling, into the viscous, receiving street below.

Signs remain after shaving and the details of male grooming,

of a surface sheen that is however concealed beneath collar and
cuffs, and my still polite and normal, business-like manner. Concern that even without my return and receipt of yet another coating
of rubber in this other parallel or whatever world, the spread of
my second, new skin, will, if it is not already, be detectable by the
most casual passing glance. To test my theory and at the same time
explore the throbbing metropolis that beckons from beyond the
office door, I walked the crowded streets in search of someone or
thing that I felt would cure my new craving for a smoother, cooler
existence. I entered a book-store in pursuit I believed of a like-
minded lady, no doubt from out of town, dressed in leather or
rubber, in stiletto-heeled boots, familiar in some way, who nevertheless seemed then to disappear into thin air after leading me
towards a shelf of magazines, one of which she touched with the
forefinger of her leather-gloved left hand, without even checking
to see if I or someone else was actually following behind her.

Drawn by its smooth packaging to this magazine titled Heel!,
printed overseas in England by Stiletto Books for the Paris offices
of the publishers and organisation also known as Heel!, I discover
between its sensual, retro-futuristic covers a description by a New
York man of a 'nocturnal visitor', Egyptian in her appearance, deadly
in her intent and treatment of his muscled physique, who follows
him home and forcibly removes him to her world by first mummi-
fying his reclining body in immobilising rubber, then submerging
him, drowning him in the water of his bath. I check the locks of
my apartment and sit through the night staring panoramically at a
changing New York, before beginning to read the strangest contents of Heel! magazine, this article sent as a letter by a female

reader and member of Heel!, expressing her criticism of a recent event or party at the Palace of Versailles.

Walking on my own in new boots as a guest to your annual celebrations in the Palace of Versailles, feeling a private pleasure in the awkwardness of their first movement and the smoothness of their changing appearance beneath the spraying light of exploding fireworks and of fountains lighted externally by flaming torch and from within the cascading jets of water, by sirens and tritons, I stood alone in contemplation and with the desire to understand what I was seeing. At the entrance to the Water Avenue which proceeds from the North Parterre to the Fountain of Neptune, I discovered for the first time the fountain of Diana's Bathing Nymphs, being a square pool with three walls adorned with sculpted figures, of which the central rectangular wall, having the appearance of a landscape from a dream, is both wide enough to accommodate a group of reclining nymphs and high enough to contain their tall naked bodies should they prefer to stand the more clearly to observe the outside world through the transparent sheet of overflowing water. Yet, until my arrival there and the distraction from their river-bank scene of the twin presence of my shining leather boots, the eleven nymphs, with a disdaining outward glance, had seemed to disregard the invitation of eleven pairs of shoes placed opposite, in front of each of their quivering, shivering forms, pretending in their splashing game that their earthly view was somehow obscured by the play of moonlight from within their world upon a silvered veil drawn across this otherworldly night. Intending, as I have said, to observe, away from the crowd, and to feel the sensual limits of my new boots, and being

unwilling at first to share these properties of mine with an outsider of whatever extreme degree of female beauty, I watched the
wriggling method of their extraction from the waters of their world
and emergence of eleven glistening women into my own in the
two minds of wonder and irritation at their immediate avoidance
of the fine footwear left before as gifts within which they were to
attend the celebration of Heel! in the Hall of Mirrors within the
palace. Besides, what language would they speak, with which to
be greeted by this dominating, incubating woman who wished in
these precious moments for no interruptions, to be left in peace,
for no human or other speech to interfere with her first commun-
ion with new and unbroken boots? Could they not just join and
accompany the reanimated statuary of children riding on swans in
the Dragon's Fountain at the other end of the tree-lined Water
Avenue emerging while I continued to study in privacy the shape
and curvature of my two reluctant new boots? And did they all
have to crowd so close, along with so many discontented Goddesses in their new shoes, arriving inevitably at this corner of the
gardens of Versailles chosen by me for its natural solitude? To which
was then added the croaking of slaves turned into frogs and the
regular, prolonged cries of agony from the Fountain of Evening.
Might I suggest that in future years, stiletto boots be placed beside the female statuary, which is surely more appropriate for a
masked ball than the court shoe. I am, however, grateful for the
mercifully quick and brutal removal by the Tourist Police of the
dancing Tai-Chi Master. Perhaps, if I may make a second request,
it would be that this scientist, unbroken at that time like my own
boots, be prevented during his imprisonment from recording the

degrees of his suffering by the provision of pen and paper, since his contributions are invariably the dullest made to your fine magazine. And perhaps the eleven nymphs might be encouraged to assist the Goddess Diana with the submersion of the new slaves at the Fountain of Evening. And there should be the clear understanding that ladies wishing to avoid the enervating and fitful appearances and disappearances through the strangely-propertied glass of the Hall of Mirrors – where one Mistress loses her treasured slave to the black night, and another receives from that unearthly source three or more devoted but unwanted slaves – should remain undisturbed through till dawn in a secluded area of the gardens where she may silently address her new boots as her own slaves, which by initiation become elevated as a part of her, being undistinguished by any separating identity from her own. In case this letter made disagreeable by the timing in the female cycle, is considered for publication, perhaps some clarification as to which or whose world the masked ball really belonged, can be printed alongside my listing of complaints. It seemed at the time to be as uncertain and changing as the appearance and ownership of my own new boots. Was I the impostor in the world of naked nymphs or were they released from their seeming dream into my version of the gardens of Versailles? The three thousand candles that lit the seventeen mirrors in the *Galerie des Glaces* and the furniture so regularly substituted served only to confuse the events of that night.

THREE

Twilight of the Gods

FEBRUARY 9TH

I was assuming, as I watched that unlikely scene, that I was viewing the night-time mating of the fire-fly from this mountain whose
identification and significance eluded me as I stood upon its summit in pyjamas with binoculars. Which of the 90 or more species
of the genus *Pyrophorus*, or as I increasingly felt, some newly evolved
species adapted to the alien nightmarish environment [into which
I had been suddenly inserted], was engaged in mating above this
pristine, red-painted version of Mexico's first great city, Teotihuacan,
which means 'Place of the Goddess'? My continued inspection of
this developing picture below, which I half suspected was the product not of swarming insects, but of a failure of my inner sight,
convinced me that several species were intermixing, probably in-
terbreeding, each of which displayed before my re-focusing
binoculars unique and distinguishing patterns of sexual behaviour.
The predominant species, in numbers not in character, rather than
emitting light through the predicted pair of conspicuous, ovoid
spots on the pronotum and from the area beneath the base of the

abdomen, appeared steadily luminous as though spheroid and bulbous like a human balloon floating passively across the night sky, but being brought to the ground by just visible [by their reflective sheen and the extension of the longest whips that coiled around the balloon shape causing a sighing sound] predators, feminine in their appearance and extremely polished like the accompanying and exoskeletal feeding beetles. Searching for the luminous organs while trying to maintain my grip on the loose stone of the mountain's lower slopes [its or her name, *Cerro Gordo*, meaning 'Fat Hill'] without removing the binoculars from in front of my glued eyes, it occurred to me that I might be observing, in the case of this singled-out species, not the mating of the adult fire-flies, but the products of their enlightened union, the eggs that in this other world, were floating perhaps through a dimensional warp into the heart of this alternate Teotihuacan Valley, being guided into its safe haven by these whip-women in stiletto-heeled boots.

The mountain on which I had arrived and at first stood, was perfectly aligned with the north-south axis of the 'Avenue of the Dead' that from the Pyramid of the Moon extends to the south in a seemingly unending straight line upon which the egg-shaped human balloons with their living contents were being landed in a queue, two by two, side by side, heading in my direction, to where I hid crouching amongst the fifteen pyramidal structures including the vast Pyramid of the Moon symbolic of the sacred mountain, *Cerro Gordo*, that loomed gigantically over the ceremonial and sacrificial proceedings. The forward propulsion along this avenue [towards the five-tiered platform fronting the Pyramid of the Moon] provided by the well-timed bull-whips of the escorting and alighting guards – who lined the avenue, equally spaced on either side of the queuing balloons, so that they stood statuesque and motionless, apart from the apparently independent action of the determined whips – brought the first in the queue into the area of the Moon Plaza, beneath the pyramid of the Goddess.

All around, appearing constantly out of the starlit night as though quite unaware of the eggs onto which they on occasion landed, squashing and extinguishing the internal light, another species of fire-fly [as I then believed them to be] was arriving in force, being in fact unmanned balloons containing an abundance of female footwear, and supplies also of bull-whips that as I watched them, hung down as though reaching for their first slithering grip of firm ground. Beyond my awareness of local custom, of the feminine inhabitants' use of the fire-fly for their personal adornment, or their easily understandable habit of keeping these luminous insects in cages in their private rooms to light their reflections and thereby contribute to the process of embellishing their beauty, I had never heard, as an enthusiastic but amateur researcher, of the requirement that the unborn insect be in some manner sacrificed like potential vermin for the appeasement or approval of the Goddess, the indwelling deity of this pyramid in front of which a swelling army of prenatal beings were assembled, congregating helplessly.

The common character of the twin species was again evident to the critical observer when, no doubt triggered by their proximity to the Moon Pyramid or by some heavenly movement [of the distant constellation of Bootes] timing their advance to birth, a number of the rubbery eggs in whose midst I had – to avoid detection by the guards positioned all about the plaza at various levels on the tiers and summits of pyramids – secreted myself, began reproducing that sighing sound heard earlier, under the same impetus provided by the encircling whips. For the first time, by removing my binoculars whose minimum focusing distance was exceeded by the close proximity of neighbouring eggs piled high and restrained by lashing whip and pyramid within the confines of the Moon Plaza, I noticed signs of real life in the interior world of the neophytic insect as if sensing that in the case of their species of destructive fire-fly the Goddess deemed that their end should precede any lively beginnings, their release into her sacred environment.

Through the translucent surface of the luminous eggs, each mimicking the condition and bound state of the excavated men buried alive within the interior of the Moon Pyramid, with hands tied behind their inclined backs [wearing collars and being each placed in front of a pyrite inlaid mirror to die by suffocation], I saw white-coated men, the fetally malformed, potential scientist, dreamers like me, struggling as I was, mouthing torrents of abuse against the Goddess. In a massive, explosive flash, followed by a huge sigh of relief and release, as if the colossal deity had herself settled upon the mound of unborn eggs and by her squatting given birth, there were produced not just the few boots generated at each sighing exhalation of the unmanned balloon, but ten thousand pairs of ugly, unevenly heeled stiletto boots that remained after the embryonic liquid of the deflated eggs had been drained from the plaza. I woke in shock, certain without daylight recourse to research notes or thesaurus, that it had been the weight of the Goddess, its consequent and terrible production of the malformed, rejected boots,

that was the sacrificial method of disposing of the unwanted geneticist [who wakes dead in his physical bed], and not the monstrous
jaws of a dream-dwelling and resurrected deity, *tyrannosaurus rex*.
I did however, this morning check my facts to the extent of confirming that the deaths of the bound sacrificial victims excavated
from the interior of the pyramid, were regulated by the position of
Venus during her 584-day celestial cycle which is of course related
to the movement of such heavenly bodies as the Constellation of
Bootes, known as Heel!.

FOUR

The Servant's Initiation

Pictures, blurred, unclear, flashing across the television screen, showing the transforming of a city, Paris. Poor quality of reception reminds me of telepathic images badly communicated. The *Place de la Concorde* with its central obelisk seemingly pushed up through the ground is alternating in its appearance between the time of the French Revolution and a future or past in which a black and polished obelisk, moonlit and occupying the same position, is surrounded by Egyptian architecture, by pyramids, pylons, temples – before reverting to the cruel, murderous scenes of the guillotining of the Queen Marie-Antoinette and several of the 2800 others killed between 1793 and 1795. Smell of blood so strong . . . I turned away from the screen reflexively, the stench follows me . . . Herd of cattle refusing to cross the *Place de la Concorde*. Sudden and successive transformations or substitutions of environment in response to our joint disgust or the leather-gloved hand of Fate: *Place de la Concorde, Place Louis XV, Place Louis XVI, Place de la Chartre*, and again the *Place de la Concorde* of modern times with its screaming traffic. The fumes enter my nostrils jolting my polluted lungs. I switch off the television, stop speaking into this recorder. The remainder of this entry is written directly down onto the journal page, the detail of the text taken from this magazine about the organisation and recruitment of Heel!, and about Paris, the last, remaining city in Europe to worship the Goddess Isis.

Obelisks symbolize the first beams of light to illuminate the world [having tall, thin, square stone shafts tapering to a pyramid-shaped peak]. Erected typically in pairs – which explains the second obelisk materialized briefly in the *Place de la Concorde* – before the entrance to a temple, their twin tips sheathed in electrum shimmer in the rays of the fierce Egyptian sun, seeming to float in the night sky above the unseen shaft, their fixed shape glowing beneath the creamy light of a full moon. They were regarded as living things, divine beings, capable of reanimation, and of regenerating the environment – when destroyed by military might or natural catastrophe – with pristine buildings made attractive by the synchronous materialization of a servant population. These new men were then entrusted with the creation of a new obelisk, this despite the Queen's knowledge of the vibrational, psychic technology by which the granite may be cut, extracted and transported from its quarry of origin, instantaneously, reappearing erect on the temple site. Considered an essential element of a servant's initiation, 'the work in the quarry was physically demanding, labour intensive and mind-numbingly repetitive. After a suitable band of rock had been identified, a series of small fires was lit and doused with water to crack the surface of the granite . . . The sides were not cut by saw – the granite was far too hard – but by teams of men rhythmically bouncing balls of dolerite [an even harder rock consisting of feld-spar and pyroxene] against the granite surface. The underside was prepared in the same exacting manner until the obelisk, at last al-most completed by this slave-labour, was supported only by isolated spurs of mother-rock . . . '

Queen Hatshepsut regarded the creation of so many new and man-made obelisks during her physical reign as pharaoh, as the most climactic achievements of her rule, requiring that their trans-port by land and by boat be painstakingly recorded in a series of illustrations on stone blocks at Karnak and on the lower south por-tico of her Deir el-Bahri temple in the Valley of the Queens. Here we are shown the 'naked obelisk' lying lashed to a sledge being towed on a sycamore wood barge towards Thebes by a fleet of twenty-seven smaller boats powered by over 850 straining oarsmen: 'Unfortunately, the flow of the Nile helps the barge on its way'. The Karnak temple, the destination of this black obelisk, 'The Most Select of Places', was connected to nearby Luxor [from which the obelisk in Paris was removed] by a processional route which was lined by sphinxes the expressive features of whom have been eroded on this our material, not ethereal plane.

During the erection in the *Place de la Concorde* of the pink gran-ite monolith, 73 feet high and weighing 220 tons, [after three years of back-breaking labour hauling the obelisk up the Nile river-bank, rowing west across the Mediterranean sea before dragging its co-lossal bulk nearly the length of France, to Paris], before a crowd of 220,000 most of whom had participated manually in its delivery, the huge winches had reached their mechanical limits with the ob-elisk not quite upright. A man's hoarse voice, drawing on his experience of slavery in Egypt, while the silent crowd holding its breath reminisced its own memories, volunteered the advice, 'Moisten the rope!'; he remembered that when left outside by his mistress in the intense desert heat, the hemp ropes would shrink as they dried, further constricting his movement, and in one life at least, causing death. In the case of Senenmut, who, though a servant to his mistress, Queen Hatshepsut, [whether his was the voice that called out from the crowd we are not informed] rose to be overseer of her labour-force of slaves, no fewer than sixty small representations of him kneeling with outstretched arms and constricted penis, have been discovered at Deir el-Bahri concealed within her temple. The accompanying short inscriptions confirm that he is engaged in worship of his mistress 'on behalf of the life, prosperity and health of the Queen of Upper and Lower Eqypt, Maatkare [Hatshepsut's throne name] living forever'. The characteristic of being immortal, the powers of self-generation and to shapeshift, are recorded in this magazine, Heel!, appearing to be the basic and natural attributes required for membership of this otherworldly organisation.

FIVE

Dark Omens

I have been reading that the architecture within the vicinity of London's 'Cleopatra's Needle', which is an obelisk like that in New York, taken apparently from the Temple of Philae in Egypt, has been similarly described by a number of commuting men as having suddenly changed in 'mid-stride' to that of 'some ancient, future time' so that for a moment they are accompanied by 'polished female beings, their heels clicking upon the sidewalk, carrying whips as though they were about to begin their work, their night duty, as priestesses to some unearthly goddess'. The unearthly sound of polished stiletto boots is simultaneously heard near the Louvre Museum in Paris, which appears to have been broken into by night, a number of empty sacks and ropes for securing wrists and ankles being found in the room housing the zodiac taken from the Temple of Denderah. The same article referred to the reporting of American tourists visiting Venice during the carnival who are themselves transported into another version of Venice, having first come into contact with women in rubber emerging from the murky waters, whose 'smooth feet are not webbed at all but rather well equipped by their defined shape and sharp heel for terrestrial living'. My copy of Heel! magazine, to which I now subscribe, contains a piece of writing by a slave of that organisation, titled *The Venetian Night* [printed verbatim below], describing the alternate existence of the Republic of Venetia which will predominate geographically and geologically over that version of Venice known to man, wiping away its previous, polluted existence like grime from a smoothed rubber boot. Included as well is a letter written by agony aunt, Madame de Morville, titled *The Denderah Vortex*, explaining the zodiac's continued use as a vortex linking Earth with the constellation of Bootes, called Heel!, by which slaves are trafficked instantaneously to that distant cosmic region.

During that cold afternoon the male porters at the San Severa hotel on the island of the Lido in the Venetian archipelago had unfolded one hundred sunbeds on the empty beach, placing each one meticulously in an evenly-spaced line, then draping over them the extravagant furs of mythic creatures whose shining black coats now brushed the raked sand on the ground beneath in the light evening breeze that blew in from the sea. It was the time of Venice's Carnival. Every year for centuries the preparations for the arrival of these female guests had been executed identically; though no sign of their nocturnal presence was yet expected. Only the few children with fantastic minds and shivering bodies suspected and questioned the silent servants about the purpose and timing of this ritual and display.

On the main island of Venice, a short journey by boat, by vaporetto, from the Lido, the riot of the multi-coloured shirt, the

American accent, the fat wallets of crude tourism, provided the casual observer with no hint to the events planned for that night. To the trained eye, perhaps, to the seer the earlier disappearance of the taxiing and ferrying gondolas, the muted sound of the singing gondoliers, evidenced the prospect of a paranormal night. While violins beside the restaurant tables of loud, ill-mannered men played on with enthusiasm forced against the knowledge of the impending hour, rubberised women drawn by the fullness of the moon from the subterranean to the mediterranean, emerged unobserved through streets of stagnant water, their glistening skin soon cloaked in darkness, their clicking heels then lost enveloped within the receiving shadow.

On the beach of the San Severa hotel, the sunbeds in their regimented row were empty pointing out to sea, the spherical moon shone brightly on the rippling water of the black lagoon, the beams of creamy ambient light revealing a vast, as yet deserted stage. As the clock-hand turned toward midnight, the reflecting surface becoming smooth, a child points at something nearly seen, his finger bent again by adult arms outstretched in fear, for rising from the sea, with open palms pressed down beside the gleaming female shape upon the healing water, a Goddess stands above the glassy sheen in testing boots that walk, then strut upon the surface, firm and sealed, towards the sloping shore.

The children, awe-struck dumb, behind drawn curtains peeping stare, wide-eyed, frozen still in fear, adult whispers hushed beside in blind despair. A second female guest arrives in curved stiletto heels and rubber, emerging perfect in the midnight light, polished, pushing up above the closing sea, the arching boots withdrawn in time, then stamping down upon the resisting, moonlit stage. While one hundred porters, with heads inclined eyes focussed to the ground, patiently kneeling wait the performance of a greeting ceremony, ancient, timeless and new, street urchins with cleaning cloth, improvising, staring, mimic for their adult years, breath taken by this posture and the vision of this overwhelming view, of dripping boots delivered, thrusting, to their care. The echoing of stiletto boot heels on solidifying water, the sound made by whips cracking in the air, by one hundred aquatic guests, clatter and smack against the stone walls and shattering window-panes of the San Severa hotel.

Elsewhere in Venetian palaces shuttered against the passage of time, the ugliness of an ignorant world, of stupid science and idiot men, evening dresses laid out upon exotic beds by nervous servants charged in the Mistress' long absence with the preservation of the priceless, timeless content of her wardrobe are secured by pin-lipped maids, transvestites, stitched tight, corsetted, bejewelled for the duration of the night. Outside, dangling down by a length of knotted rope from the balcony into the muddy depths of the foul-smelling canal below, the rubbery boot-slave, subconscious, weighted down, animation suspended for the year, is hoisted by her leather opera-gloves clear from the polluted water into which is lowered for the night the Mistress' rubber clothing, preserved in substitution, undetected by the outsider's curious eye.

Slapped by the Mistress' dark-skinned glove into sudden recognition of his rôle as slave, she observes him at her feet, her whip for now withheld behind her back, though serpent coils, candle-lit, inquisitive, remain in sight upon the marble floor, reminding constantly of his most likely fate, the irreversibility of this natural state. His feverish body so recently revived, previously kneeling beaten about the face, polishes, unable yet to stop and breathe, prostrated there beneath the reflection, flickering and otherworldly, of his Mistress' sculpted shape, of her white face impassive behind the haughty, leathered mask, behind the intervening sheet of glass. His annual duty so painstakingly performed beneath her silent gaze is duplicated a thousand times upon the shine of marble stones of palaces unshuttered for this single night, by boot-slaves lifted from the Adriatic sea, the social detritus of science raised prematurely from the seeming dead.

The sound of music, of vital violins and of drunken, gesturing men, wafted in the deepening night, slows perceptibly to the Mistress' ear; the motion of the revelling tourist then seized, frozen mid-step, the movement of his travelling body held in abeyance, expressing sudden disbelief, is fixed in helpless admiration of the passing ladies, their faces masked and cloaked in black, who move between them, touching with their outstretched whips, overbalancing with extended leather glove or forcing boot. Upon the water, frozen still in time, its creamy surface firm to the tread of female heel and the feet of dancing monkeys on taut leashes, from the nearby island of the Lido the guests of the San Severa hotel in rubber masks and black-hooded fur converge in cruel conversation upon the appointed hour, upon the steps of the white-stoned balustraded bridge that by the moonlight lead on past the pink marble facade of the Doge's palace, to the prison.

A shiver, an earthquake's tremor vibrating blurs the focus of this otherwordly and inhuman scene where man and monkey mix and play; the ivory moonlit sea becomes as rigid ice and as stalactites drips water on the rubbered heads of weeping slaves that kneeling hang with death beside the snowbound palace, necks locked together by enchanting spell and frozen chain within the eternal night. The architecture, composite, intermediate between two worlds, adjusted by this shudder appears resolved, the focus tightening, the clarity restored. The boorish tourist is converted from his vulgar state, transformed from his immobilized, stunned, unblinking state, his lifeless living torso becomes incorporated in hardening rubber polished black, his flexing arms are linked behind with glowing cuffs of cooling steel, his lower body fixed embedded within the pink-stoned walls, and set within the chiselled mantel of internal fires that blaze against the blizzard's cold.

On the pavement below the Doge's palace, crossed over from the thirteenth century when Venice's dreaded and infamous Tourist Police, the Council of Ten's instrument for torture and repression, cast a shadow across her maritime empire, a number of tethered ape-like men, spread out like dogs on radial leads, comb and then sift the blanketing snow for litter, refuse, for objects materialised from their world, beneath the overseer's guiding whip, the lashing of her foreign tongue. Ropes of stretching elastic rubber lowered like fishing-line from the palaces of the Grand Canal, from the fifteenth century facade of the Ca'd'Oro, twitch above the frozen surface, as signs of human life, of the boot-slave polishing in a fever, his outline seen fleetingly beneath the ice, beneath the reclining figure of his leather-booted Mistress, ensure the smooth progress of her gondola beyond the Rialto bridge, the punctual timing of her masked entrance to the Doge's palace.

Opposite the water-gate of the palace adjoining the Ca'd'Oro, pushing up through thinning, snow-covered ice beneath which a second boot-slave invisibly labours, a circular mooring-pole capped with a human form, seemingly impaled by some monster from the deep, then dipped in molten rubber and left in agony to die, looks up religiously to the balcony where the Mistress stands imperious in noble dress, her patient whip dangling from a leather opera-glove, her waiting gondola lashed tight about his stiffened neck. She is Diane de Poitiers, one of the five members, each counted twice, with and without the obscuring leather mask, who compose the Council of Ten, the supreme leaders of the Republic of Venetia, who meet once a year at midnight at the Doge's palace, on Carnival night, to elect from their number and to crown her, *La Serenissima*, Bride of the Adriatic.

Inside the Doge's palace, the medieval 'Palace of Justice' with its 'court of the room of the Cord', which is the seat of government, the organising centre of Heel!, where plans are made behind our patriarchal scene, decisions taken for this modern version of their world, four of the five, twin-faced Council members, Nefertiti, Semiramis, Cleopatra and Helen of Troy, deliberate about the pressing problems of that other tourist-infested Venice, cushioned on human furniture with ears removed smoothed over by encasing rubber. The questions raised: How and with what numbers to re-introduce the Tourist Police so essential for the preservation of their world; when and with what means to obliterate the nineteenth century causeway and the hideous factories of the adjoining mainland, to secure the outer bounds and good health of the Venetian city-state; what manpower, kneeling or temporarily erect, is required to dismantle the white concrete railway station constructed in 1954? After which it is unanimously agreed, before her imminent, de-layed arrival at the grand entrance to the palace, at the ceremonial 'Giant's Staircase' where the gods, Mars and Neptune, were turned spell-bound to stone in 1567, that after a confirming inspection of the two huge globes and the walls covered with the maps of the two worlds in the *Sala dello Scudo*, Diane de Poitiers is to be elected for the period of one year, *La Serenissima*, Bride of the Adriatic, in recognition and for the purpose of the most rapid expansion of the circulation of the Paris-based Heel! magazine.

Crowned between the statues of Mars and Neptune with a cres-cent moon upturned upon the head-dress that surrounds her leather mask, receiving from the extended glove of Semiramis the bow and quiver of the Moon Goddess, Diana, the foundress of Venetia, then responding to the loud whip-cracks and smacking gloves of the thousand masked members of the Great Council by her pun-ishment of the kneeling Casanova, Diane de Poitiers turns to enter the palace followed in procession by the Council of Ten and the members of the Great Council who file ceremonially past the fresco of 'The Coronation of the Virgin' in the *Sala del Guariento* on the second floor, into the *Sala del Maggior Consiglio*. Once inside the Hall of the Great Council, a chamber of monumental proportions, Diane de Poitiers, *La Serenissima*, takes up her position on the bal-cony overlooking the frozen lagoon where three riderless horses are seen dragging at speed a giant cage filled with flaming wood, spiralling away from a central point marked by a boot-heel, equi-distant from the Doge's palace and the island of San Giorgio Maggiore, in an ever-widening arc, finally mapping out a melted circle of vast circumference equal in area to that lit up by the beaming shafts of descending moonlight.

Below the balcony, the hundred guests of the San Severa hotel, dressed and masked in rubber, cloaked in fur, the Tourist Police, play cat and mouse with a prisoner just released, undressed in stages, redressed in black rubber, from head to foot, a trident pressed into his right hand, his body then held in place, brought shivering to its knees. The nature of his crime, the sentence passed, is read out slowly by Cleopatra, the retiring 'Bride of the Adriatic', who condemns at length the corrupting and damaging effect on the built and moral fabric of the Republic of Venetia of this civil servant's slogan, 'Veni etiam', interpreted as, 'Come again and again'. As proof, the erect body of Casanova, the salt-smuggling philanderer, is shown, then thrown from the balcony for its examination beneath the vicious boots of the Tourist Police. With her bow strained and accurately aimed at the heart of the cringing and protesting prisoner, a flaming torch guiding the flight of the burning arrow to its fleshy target, Diane de Poitiers has slain her quarry, pierced him through and dumped him dead upon the bleeding snow. Pulled to his feet, and lifted sagging in the air, his body is tossed into the canal by rubbered Amazonian hands, over the balustrade of the *Ponte della Paglia*.

SIX

The End of Politics

It seems that I am not alone with my incongruous sightings of polished women in Egyptian dress in the streets of New York, or my repeated visions of those sections of familiar buildings whose nocturnal transformations linger into the day before the editing and reasoning eye has deleted them from my re-focused view. Even the most sacred of our nation's monuments are not immune from these sickening influences. The following when taken in context with each other rather than dismissed as the delusions of eccentric men, takers of hallucinogens, create new and bewildering certainties in the reflective mind concerned with rational interpretations, the most likely of explanations, the balance of probabilities and so forth. Is there by some unpredicted chance an attempt being made by an alien and feminine force to first psychically invade and then physically overcome what remains of the male of our species? It appears from the reports of recent events below that the impact is both geological and cultural as if no stone is to be left unturned or in its sculpted state without its transmogrification by rubber. Not only do I read of and see on the television screen examples of Earthly women upon whom a man might have expected to rely in a tight corner, who are flaunting their mimicking of this new Egyptian fashion of dress, or the leather catsuit with its distinguishing HEEL! logo, and, if this is to be really believed, seeking to switch allegiance to this outlandish organisation of the stiletto-heeled invader, but also, a number of influential men succumbing in no time to the pressure brought to bear by the heel upon mind and numbed body [so that they are enslaved even before the struggle is begun], collaborate with the divinely feminine enemy undermining whatever firmness of purpose exists in the militarily-minded, fighting man upon whom we must rely for final protection. Indeed, what may have been understood as evidence of a battling of two opposed factions – the ebbing and flowing of the superficial layer of black rubber from which the alien army emerges each night, [which is by day overwhelmed by a return to the rubberless routine and normality of city life, and is dismissed as psychological and sensual aberration], is today in the media acknowledged to be evidence of a battle already lost with a return to sexual slavery its unspoken consequence. Only the unpaid shoe-shine boy who is as the result of this onslaught engineered by polished boot and herding whip, now in the majority, can possibly celebrate the rubberizing of his soon anonymous identity, the effective castration of values fought and picked over by victor and vulture in the military history of war and its campaigning for predominance of an ideal which has seemingly become in the modern, evolved man just and inevitably an absolute appreciation of feminine beauty of form and dress [for which no other cause seems worth the fight, or reason for the preservation of usual identity].

1. Appallingly, against all that is right and good, but witnessed by the unlying camera, the unbiased and still free news-reporter, as well as the house-bound, rope-bound man with the panoramic view, his male neighbour who is sitting or kneeling out this external catastrophe [which threatens his mind at every post-pubescent turn], that symbol of universal freedom for which so much innocent blood was spilt in the cause of her safe preservation, the Statue of Liberty, the 151-foot, 226-ton statue constructed magnificently from a shell of copper plates bolted to Eiffel's steel frame, was seen in the night to change her appearance as though vanity at last takes precedence over the finest principle. The lapping water, its growing viscosity, rose slowly up the draping folds of her classic dress, so that finally when her black silhouette was exposed by a full moon emerged from behind the cover of thick cloud, a sheen of gleaming surface rubber coated fetishistically the skin of this once reliable friend. The gentlest wind blew to reveal the nauseating shape, the exaggerated height and curve of a concealed stiletto heel, together with the reforming chains of man's immanent and future slavery. Her torch of freedom held so proudly, so tirelessly and for so long, was extinguished without a fight by the same sea-breeze, as if with her own glad co-operation. The pages of a book [into which the tablet held in her other reflective hand was transformed as if by the intention of this now living goddess] fell fluttering down to the thickening water revealing its title to have been none other than that published [by that most decadent and reprehensible of organisations, Stiletto Books] for the Paris offices of Heel!, *Slaves of Isis*. Is the still rational man to conclude from the excessive enthusiasm of her apparent creator, the French sculptor anagrammatically

named Bartholdi, that he was an early collaborator with the organisation, Heel!, intending not a gift for the American people but to deliver instead a modern equivalent of the Trojan Horse? Were not the pages turned in their downward flight to rubber, to be then used as rafts by the invading army lurking within the body of the statue transported previously from the distant constellation of Bootes?

2. Further to yesterday's reporting of the translucent, glowing balloons loaded with their shocking cargo of stiletto-heeled boots, that were believed to have descended from the etheric or astral plane onto the dark water of the man-made lake beside that great tribute to the 'Father of our Country', the Washington Monument, we are being advised to stay indoors, that some organic trap-door on the submerged bottom of the wicker-basket timed to release both boot and whip from the unmanned craft, has equipped an army of 'dripping rubber-women' for a full-frontal attack on Capitol Hill. Last weekend a group of tourists descending the 897 steps in the interior of the 555-feet high obelisk, briefly disappeared down an extra flight of 'extremely polished steps into a watery, rubbery otherworld where women dressed in leather or rubber, reclined on compacted male cushions made apparently from the same material . . . Beside them more faceless slave-men kneeling as if for an eternity, their heads naturally inclined by a flap of neck-skin linking chest to chin, attentive to the future needs of their sleeping mistresses, gradually stirred before us as though in response to the chiming of an unseen, even more unreal clock'. [The contributors to the report, the men interviewed on their return, on re-scaling the invisible flight of steps, were described as having disagreed

amongst their bewildered selves as to whether the polished leather said to cover the women's bodies was not in some or most cases made in fact of rubber]. It appears that last night bolts of lightning that for the micro-second linked our planet with that in some unnamed constellation [the constellation of Bootes] were transmitted down through the aluminium pyramid at the top of the obelisk, deep into the Washington ground, the electrification of which, according to the reasoning given, must have revived this hibernating army and by a process of spasmodic resuscitation provided the energy by which the black, enlivened and shining bodies then launched their lethal attack on Capitol Hill, on the most industrious of our nation's late-sitting politicians and impartial observers. Clearly discernible in the news footage shown this morning, their polished exoskeletal bodies contrasting like those of their riders and the advancing foot-soldiers below with the white marble stone of the besieged Capitol, huge scarab-beetles pluck suited men from the ground, disappearing beyond the searchlights, back into the overcast, rain-filled night. Their job completed, descending the steps as a regimented unit, the booted foot-soldiers, discarding their still wriggling whips, also disappear as suddenly into the enveloping darkness, the sound of heels lingering briefly behind them.

3. Both the Grand Canyon and the San Andreas fault are reported this morning to be filling with and oozing black rubber of the same viscosity that continues to grow on the masonry of the Capitol, as though the consciousness of planet Earth, the Goddess herself, conspires with these materializing and alien women seeking to rid herself finally of the pollution and memory of man. I read that the

completion of the construction of the obelisk, the Washington Monument, was delayed for a considerable period of time while stone that was deemed sufficiently pink was located and approved before quarrying [by whom? The membership and organisation of Heel!?]. The cities of San Francisco and Los Angeles are also subject to the nightly attacks by scarab-beetles and the transformations of architecture and environment experienced elsewhere. The oceans viewed from satellites appear smooth and black, the whole planet like the polished moonlit head of the new species of rubberman, except that no rotation of the latter is permitted by the tethering rope or restraining chain.

SEVEN

Death of the Patriarchs

MARCH 15TH

Read the following account while lying prone [face down rather than in the more usual supine position] and sleepy-eyed in my New York bed, written in 1894 by Frenchman, Edouard Naville. The book from which the text below is quoted verbatim is titled precociously, *The Temple of Deir el-Bahri: its plan, its founders and its first explorers: Introductory Memoir*. Having finished this much of the page I fell asleep, my face falling forwards onto a torch-lit picture of the painted interior of Queen Hatshepsut's mortuary temple near Thebes, in Egypt's Valley of the Queens. Simultaneously, I felt a rustling sensation within my forehead, observed the shape blurred by the intense desert heat of a shimmering, black granite pyramid [which seemed to be a great distance away in the back of my head], together with dim memories of other lives. I had lost consciousness at or just before midnight, becoming aware and normally alert, regaining a full sense of myself, suddenly in the otherworld of dreams and nightmare.

The tourists who annually swarm into Thebes seldom depart from the ancient city of Amen without visiting the magnificent natural amphitheatre of Deir el-Bahri, where the hills of the Libyan range present their most imposing aspect. Leaving the plain by a narrow gorge, whose walls of naked rock are honey-combed with tombs, the traveller emerges into a wide open space bounded at its furthest end by a semi-circular wall of cliffs. These cliffs of white limestone, which time and sun have coloured rosy yellow, form an absolutely vertical barrier. They are accessible only from the north by a steep and difficult path leading to the summit of the ridge that divides Deir el-Bahri from the wild and desolate Valley of the Tombs of the Kings. Built against these cliffs, and even as it were rooted into their sides by subterranean chambers, is the temple of which Mariette said that 'it is an exception and accident in the architectural life of Egypt'.

But perhaps not in the nocturnal life of Egypt . . . Pinched between the serrated forelegs of a riderless scarab-beetle, I was woken as well by the whirring of its polished wings whose rapid beating produced the effect of air-conditioning on my naked dangling body warmed into a sweat by the North African Mediterranean night. Behind me, by a twist of my neck, I could see the Straits of Gibraltar through which presumably at the same great speed – as if late for an event at which we would be the last to arrive – we had just flown at a height which in a cooler month would have been on collision course with the southward migration of the swallow, sacred bird of the Goddess Isis. No sooner, it seemed, had I returned by the completion of my rubbery neck's rotation, my head to its forward position, than I beheld [to borrow from the dated vocabulary common to those first explorers of the Egyptian monument –

whether they were the time-travellers of dreams or that variety of the modern plodding and dusting Egyptologist, for example J.R. Buttles, author of *The Queens of Egypt* and the following lines] . . . I beheld Queen Hatshepsut's temple, *Djeser Djeseru*, 'Holiest of the Holy', a part of which, like the astronomical ceiling of the Temple of Denderah, has been removed, dug up by the French patriarch [to be exhibited as a trophy in the museum of the Louvre].

It is built at the base of the rugged Theban cliffs, and commands the plain in magnificent fashion; its white colonnades rising, terrace above terrace, until it is backed by the golden living rock. The ivory white walls of courts, side chambers and colonnades, have polished surfaces which give an alabaster-like effect. They are carved with a fine art, figures and hieroglyphs being filled in with rich yellow colour, the glow of which against the white gives an effect of warmth and beauty quite indescribable.

Below me, being focused by the new rhythm of the scarab-beetle's beating wings, the hovering of its body above the moonlit Valley of the Queens strewn with the litter of helicopter parts smoking in defeat, I perceived the temple plan studied earlier in bed, spread out in its original pristine condition with those elements – the man-made pools of dark water gleaming in the cream-coloured Egyptian light, the fragrant trees, their scent wafting up to me despite the stench of burnt oil – that had been omitted from the mundane accounts of the academic writer. The cliffs behind appeared to me almost white, a striking contrast with the sheen of the scarab-beetle, the polished black shine of the Heel! troops dealing on the ground with each fleeing pilot brought down by the grappling legs and crunching mouth-parts of intercepting beetles, several of which settled greedily beside their prey on the valley floor reluctantly quitting their kill when lashed by coiling whips about their sensitive antennae.

Registering no doubt the same information as its human passenger, but from the perspective of a scarab-beetle observing the final, climactic skirmishes in the flaming night sky between outmanoeuvred helicopter-pilots and the exoskeletally armoured beetles hunting in disciplined packs, each with eight or nine adults, one being ridden and given direction by a member of Heel!, my hovering and apparently two-minded, six-legged transport for the duration of this very real-seeming dream [it being uncertain whether to release my body and join in the fighting or to complete our journey into the interior of the temple], finally, in a diving swoop which took us low over the three ascending terraces, over the open-air stairway marked out by pairs of opposing granite sphinxes, entered the cool of the hypostyle hall flying between colossal kneeling statues leading through hollowed rock to a second torch-lit chamber, to the Hall of Judgement. A whip directed from below at its vulnerable undercarriage caused the hovering beetle to drop me, at the same time waking me to the familiar world of my New York apartment. I did, however, remain dreaming long enough to see chained against the statues outside or being sentenced within the Hall of Judgement, those male politicians listed as missing after the attack upon Capitol Hill. I have also noted while this morning researching the area of the Valley of the Queens that restoration of the roofless hypostyle hall which had appeared newly built and in perfect condition, is being undertaken by some Polish ladies, doubtless themselves encased in the leather or rubber clothing characteristic of the member of Heel!.

EIGHT

The Metaphysics of War

MARCH 16TH

Secured to my chair which is in turn secured to my apartment floor, projecting my thoughts and dream images of Egypt onto the rectangular screen of my balcony window, I am about to review the memorized scenes of hand-to-leg fighting, between scarab-beetle and man, and the tactics employed by American helicopters in their failed attempt to free the world leaders from the Temple of Queen Hatshepsut. The precaution and option of bondage, a measure that may dismay the reader who has discovered my half-eaten, half-starved body before the pages of this journal, is explained not by any final admission of guilt, of a new liking, my conversion to the life and fashions of Heel!, but the rational and very real concern that the scarab-beetles re-envisioned by me and therefore somewhat controlled by my re-creation of their flight, might unbeknownst to me, by some new tactic, include within their burgeoning numbers, their New York relatives, the immediate and unpredictable presence of which could result in my removal into their world.

It is therefore precisely the beetles' ability to appear suddenly and in locations to which they seem not to have previously flown that is the reason of my study of their movements, indeed their comings-and-goings in the Valley of the Queens, against which the state-of-the-art helicopter regardless of firepower and 360-degree vision, appears invariably vulnerable. Replaying combat scenes before my mind's eye, it soon becomes apparent it is not the cover of darkness that has defeated the radar and western technology of the helicopter, but the beetle's possession of a cloak of invisibility, its capacity to dematerialize its insectoid physique avoiding detection and the travelling bullet, and the complimentary faculty of conjuring up form from some dimension to which it tactically retreats, withdrawing itself temporarily from the field of battle before lethally returning and inserting the armoured leg amongst the rotating blades.

Such mystifying and unpredictable behaviour suggests to my stilled mind that freezes the past moment as completely as my bound body is immobilised by knotted rope in the present [moment, which draws by its rubbery nakedness the voyeuristic attention and un-wanted applause of New York's first female converts to the Heel! cause], some precognitive capability within the cellular conscious-ness of the emerging beetle, perhaps itself contributing to the scarab-beetle's accurate projection of the helicopter's precise coor-dinates, even my own now, seated as bait during this scientific investigation. The helicopter attempting to pursue the beetle in its inter-dimensional manoeuvring reappears after becoming partially invisible, with its metal exoskeleton crippled, the blades tangled in a molten jumble, the pilots' flesh joined up, orifices sealed shut, a rubbery reflection of the agricultural phenomenon whereby, when an environmental threshold is at last reached, engineering with genes leads to a rubberizing distortion in the pulsing motion into and out of physical space of the nutritious food-crop, as is reportedly the unhealthy case today.

The change of appearance of my television screen in the foreground of my apartment, interrupts my interior speculation as to the metaphysics of war, this struggle between opposing forces, with an announcement whose wording I can barely hear or report due to the low setting of volume prior to the roping of my torso which allows the freedom to write wristily and no more. The familiar newsreader fails in his repeated effort to communicate due to the leather blinding-hood, a product and adaptation of medieval falconry, with its plume of feathers, that encases all but his aquiline nose, his arms being gathered like clipped, featherless wings behind him. Instead, this picture switches after a brief interval, [some point being proved to the male viewer by this delay], from the silenced man to a group of women dressed as I have just observed them in my frame-by-frame replaying of my flight within the Hall of Judgement of the Temple of Queen Hatshepsut.

'Good evening . . . please forgive this interruption and substitution of your usual televised entertainment. I trust you find our appearance within the privacy of your homes at least as visually appealing as the programmes whose transmission and broadcast we have temporarily blocked and suspended. We ask you not to move from your seats, not to fear our presence, nor attempt perversely to change channels during this brief intermission; you will find that we reappear on each and every programme that you select. Accept our intrusion into your lives and expect this technical performance to be repeated without warning at any time in your future. Normally we will be specifying the timing of each of our successive visits to your domestic and very personal world when you will each be required to be our welcoming host. We hope that you will each look forward, even with trepidation, to our arrival in your home, whether through this medium or on occasion, perhaps when provoked or suspicious of your correct response to our words, through the front door. Expect the knock of the rubber-gloved fist or the kick of the stiletto boot and be assured that we will rectify without delay whatever omission or laxness or irreverence in your behaviour that has been detected by the members of Heel!.

We are the Council of Ten from the other world of Venetia. We are seated here opposite you at this long table so that you might join with us at this the last supper of your previous life prior to your gradual and certain transformation at our hands and booted feet from which you will each be resurrected in the knowledge that you have been initiated into the transdimensional realms of the Venetian empire as slaves of the Goddess Isis, a purpose for which your long evolution under our supervising gaze has equipped you perfectly. You may begin to recognize who we are, when we remove our masks and your amazement begins to subside into silent, natural awe of the sculpted beauty of our facial features and highly-polished figures. You may begin to remember who we are as historical figures from your distant past or, if your memories have been trained to bridge that divide, from the dream that you may have experienced last night. We are Semiramis of Ancient Babylon, Nefertiti and Cleopatra of Ancient Egypt, Diane of French Poitiers, and Helen of Troy. Our bodies are transfigured from semi-divine to the divinity of the immortal Goddess Isis.

Kneel before us as slaves and celebrate this fulfilment of destiny for which you and your star-gazing ancestors have waited so long. Raise your glasses filled with red wine or whatever you have in your hand, and drink with us to your future in worlds where our clothing, inevitably strange to your normal sight, with our tall rubber head-dresses and these heels so high as to seem impossibly unreal to you mortal men, is the cause of instant worship and endless sacrifice. Please ignore our whips that we have brought carelessly to the supper-table unless you believe that fate accepted by gods and stars alike, is on this occasion to be challenged by your puny male might. Then fear our presence and the timing of our return to your mundane world. Good evening, slaves, and thank you for inviting us to join you at your last supper.'

NINE

Teatro Amazonas

Woken by the sound of the order being given to evacuate these
seedy Parisian premises; yet it was spoken as a greeting by a male
voice, that of 'Ausmann' or as I have this morning just confirmed,
Haussmann, my companion of the night during our lengthy prom-
enade through emptied boulevards re-planted by the industry of
rubbermen whose anonymous physiques more nearly resembled
my own than that of the nineteenth-century dress of this French
man of clearly Germanic origins. He had, as his interminable
monologue forcefully conveyed to me while I accompanied him
reluctantly through avenues of newly planted rubber trees [named
in Latin, *palmetto stiletto*], once been, during the time of the Empire, in full charge of laying out the Bois de Boulogne, the provision
of a healthy water supply, also a gigantic system of sewers which
were, like the Seine itself, to which he now pointed with the most
exaggerated and Teutonic gestures, filled by the blackest liquid, its
overflowing smoothness gleaming in the full moonlight as the creator of Paris' opera-house was sucked still gesticulating defiantly

beneath its slow-moving, rubbery mass.

Finding myself within the vicinity of the Eiffel Tower, its obvious priapic ambitions for which I had felt a tourist's affinity during my pubescent travels, I observed from a distance, being by then rather well camouflaged by the same black liquid, a group of voluptuously curving, most feminine, but rubber-clad ladies any description of whose sculptural beauty must of necessity include every superlative attributed by Monsieur Haussmann to each of his own creations and embellishments of this most romantic of northern cities. Stealthily, after their sudden and quite inexplicable disappearance into the thin night air [that had nevertheless felt and appeared to thicken by degrees in proportion to the rising of the level of rubbery water, so that my lungs as well as my skin seemed to be functioning naturally in the new conditions], I approached with furtive movements, emerging from and sinking back into the environing rubber that lapped at the four curved legs supporting the Eiffel Tower.

Confirming on my safe and unnoticed [subsequently contradicted by experience] arrival beneath the overwhelming structure of soon-to-be rubberized iron that the female objects of my riveted and unblinking attention had disappeared without leaving any rubbery trace or metallic echo of stilettos, I had for the first time since listening to the architectural descriptions of Haussmann, realised that of my two addresses, in Paris and New York, the latter though far distant from this very real-seeming European city, was the more authentic in terms of solidity and predictability. I was at this time of wavering and disbelief in the complete existence of my Parisian surroundings, even the vast structure, its rubber bulk that was sheltering me from the first drops of rain which was delivered instead as a steady stream of rubber pellets [which seamlessly joined the lava-like flow of black living liquid that held me knee-deep and almost immobile beneath the thousands of interlocking girders that climbed skyward above me], suddenly removed from my environment shared with the ever-toiling rubbermen and the stiletto trees as I reached with outstretched arms to escape upwards.

Transported in this instant not to New York but to South America, I found myself gripping in my slippery hands the chain of a French chandelier [brought with me?] and seated clumsily amongst its lighted crystals, being immediately terrified of falling from the ceiling of the auditorium of this Amazonian opera-house and of my imminent death amongst the rows of caned seats occupied by identically dressed and equally rubber-clad ladies below. Instead I was being slowly lowered by the chain's extension [a manoeuvre reserved normally only for the purpose of the chandelier's cleaning and polishing] until to my astonishment, the four rubberized legs of the Eiffel Tower, enclosing a circle at the centre of which had been the chandelier, became visible imprinted upon the curving surface of the dome, becoming gradually clearer as I moved in my perilous descent ever nearer to and eventually within range of the flailing whips of the irate and most thoroughly polished audience.

I should add, in case this journal – as it is my intention in recording these experiences – finds its way into the rubberless hands of a surviving academic, that I passed three tiers containing ninety boxes with five seats in each, filled to capacity with the static and observing figures of rubber- or leather-clad goddesses. In addition, the stage curtain which was made out of stiff canvas and depicted

the 'Meeting of the Waters' of the Negro and Solimoes rivers [form-
ing the Amazon river], was being raised during my descent and
beneath its portrayal of Goddess Yara, 'Mother of the Waters', reclining in a shell wearing protective rubber, I observed on stage –
presumably there as an aid to the singing of some operatic aria, a
theatrical prop related to this rubbery theme – the stiletto boots,
huge and polished black, still dripping river water, of perhaps the
as yet unseen diva, at which time the silence was broken not just by
the serpentine cracking of impatient whips, but the exclaiming so
loud that it woke me from my dreaming sleep, of the single or pair
of words, 'Manaus!' [which is also the Portuguese name, in our
regular world of usual happenings, of the city the famed opera-
house of which, *Teatro Amazonas*, lies at the very entrance to the
mythologic and interior world of the Amazonian forest].

TEN

Cinderella's Shoe

MARCH 24TH

My physical body is pulled elastically after my dream body into a dream or intermediate etheric environment. The outside, the pink facade of the opera-house, *Teatro Amazonas*, in Brazil's city of Manaus, appears as it looks in the photographs that I have seen during my research, with significant differences. The black driveway beneath my bedroom feet feels made from that smooth blend of wild rubber [tapped by those rubber slaves released from kind dreams into this jungle world], clay and sand, intended to dampen the noise and surprised cries of men and horses, of the carriages that they in turn pull. The sidewalks of the sleeping city are as predicted in my note-taking, constructed from the same convenient raw materials, upon which tramp the chained dreaming slaves returned in the same fashion as I, for their nocturnal, moonlit labouring, the unconscious collection of rubber, a material from which they increasingly seem to be made. The simian flexibility of their limbs becomes weighed down by shackles, the burden of their growing consciouness within this alternate world, their forgetfulness of the world that I can still remember. Unchained and therefore as I am relatively fleet of foot and as yet unseen by the rubber-clad booted guards who provide direction and purpose to the returning male slaves, I explore in full alertness, cautiously, the area surrounding the opera-house.

Moving agilely amongst the concealing shadows in this, my newly rubberized body, in Saint Sebastian's square, behind the live target of Amazonian archers, the twitching body of whom betrays his previous freedom and adventurous spirit, a night-dreamer like me, I discover the Palace of Justice the architecture of which mimicks in small scale but quite recognisably that of the Palace of Versailles from whose Hall of Mirrors I have been projected, in the manner and by means advised in a back issue of Heel! magazine. The Municipal Market appears as expected as a replica of Paris' *Les Halles* where varieties of the female boot are sold imported by night in the slave-driven cargo ships anchored against the floating dock, beyond which on the opposite bank of the black viscous waters of the Rio Negro stretch endlessly the rubber plantations, the destiny and nation of preselected rubber slaves.

Had I not seen in New York's expensive avenues, walking in the elegant, tree-lined boulevards of Paris, appearing incongruous by their otherworldly strange beauty the polished ladies with their beguiling smiles and those stiletto boots recruiting restless, sleepless men like me? Hearing a high-pitched sound emanating from within the opera-house, from the auditorium of which I had almost seen the human, stiletto-booted form of the Goddess – the consciousness of whom, I now believe is within the spreading rubber sheen that is covering the earthly world – I turn my back on the

smooth, moonlit surface of the Rio Negro and in a straight line,
since the physical houses shown in my research do not exist and
intervene in this other world, on all fours [with my figurative tail
still between my legs and my wagging tongue testing my rubbery
cheeks as is often the male and natural way here in Manaus], I arrive upon the black-and-white terrace with its wavy, serpentine
patterning, in front of the *Teatro Amazonas*.

No sooner had I, judging myself to be alone, raised myself up
to my civilised height, than the ground, which was somehow under the vibrational influence of the diva's voice, began itself to ripple
like the disturbed *Rio Negro*, so that it seemed to be a continuation
of the uncertain and viscous waters of the nearby river. When its
appearance of solidity, upon which I could again rely for balance
on two legs, resumed [the patterning of waves being fixed apparently and permanently in place], I noted by my painstaking
observations – my delighting in detail characteristic of the highly
paid academic – the exact and minute detail and new appearance of
what had in fact just materialized before me, a Cinderella-like car-
riage, a chariot drawn by human horses from which emerges . . . a
spectacularly beautiful woman, a goddess whose immaculate and
booted impression now justifies the routine suffering of these
whipped, blinkered men. I follow her, pretending to have arrived
with her, holding the train of her French dress, entering in this
fashion after her into the auditorium where I immediately note
[letting go of the dress in order to write in my note-book from
which this journal entry is derived] that the caned chairs have been
replaced by red velvet, that the feminine audience – except for the
rubber-clad guards at the doors and patrolling in high-heeled boots

the blood-red carpet in the aisle – are similarly dressed. I wake in my New York bed, in shock, to the repeated shouting from close quarters of the familiar word or words, 'Manaus!'.

Footnote: It is not clear to the publishers whether his ejection from the opera-house was the consequence of his seeming to search for the stiletto-heeled shoe or boot beneath the skirt of the dress, or his note-taking which revealed him not to be the diligent servant after all, or the objectionable fact of his sex being that of a man.

ELEVEN

The Revelation

Sitting in the darkness. Spotlit by a shaft of light angled through the glass of my window, transfixing me, impressing mental states and imagery upon me, projecting me bodily within the rectangular space in front of me. Mental muscles are being flexed, becoming increasingly spring-like as I am moved back and forth through planes of existence, both physical and alien, experiencing visions of cities, unearthly landscapes and strange worlds far beyond the etheric environments to which I am already accustomed. Rhythmically, I am pulled back into a primary reality where the areas and volumes of geometry, the angles of trigonometry are perceived without shape, as original mathematical ideas prior to their dimensional birthing in sensual worlds. Buffeted by vibrational winds, scattered through empty, potential universes, swarming alphabets of living and death, of genetic still letterless letters, take form, materializing my new skin smoothed by the cooling currents, the womb-like pressures of an emerging world.

The sound of chisel on rock struck by an invisible hand, the

three-dimensional echo of stiletto heels on flagstones, the feel of
the leather glove, the whip, project me from my window-seat, conscious within another world, upon some museum floor. The
repeated sound delivered to my securely bound and seated body
from a third, further, yet more remote world, penetrates deep into
my newly formed, stillborn and entombing skull, trepanning its
bone, splintering my thought into individualised words, their
meaning and composition unclear, confused: 'Opus sine . . . Opus
sin . . . Pous sin . . . Poussin . . . Poussin . . . ' The muffled cries of
tied and sacked men being dragged over flagstones behind me,
cease, and in the silent museum's gloom the chisel resumes its patient work, in front of me, within the two-dimensional flat picture
space, its firm target a tomb upon whose surface is being painstakingly inscribed beneath the moonlight, under the flickering first
stars, by the kneeling man, the painting's rough artisan, the words:
'ET IN ARCADIA EGO'. Beside him, standing, overseeing, stiletto-heeled, a shepherdess but dressed in leather being slowly
polished by the new moon, is the Goddess, fabricator through her
manual agents, of the known and knowing world. She looks in-
wards within the framed, fixed space which is suddenly transformed
by her directing eye, by orders given to enlivened men, their purpose to serve beneath the gravity of her boot, the spiralling
whip that cracks across the canvas's, my window's night sky. She
breathes air into their empty lifeless lungs, the slave's vocabulary
deep into their brainless skulls, until with new lips they stammer
uncertain into free speech, their rubbery mouths being then
undemocratically sealed by the priestess member of Heel!. They
appear a new breed of boot-slave which is fated by astrology, by

some distant constellation, to live immortally in blind, everlasting service to this Goddess, their undying obedience to the organisation of Heel! seeming to this observer to be innately guaranteed.

The man, kneeling, ready to stand, resisting, the chisel restless in his peasant's hand, delays, looks up sideways, gazing upon the Goddess' polished stiletto boot. My male consciousness flickers back into that primal, sightless world until the sound of bull-whip upon the sculptor's protesting flesh restores my vision of this transforming scene, where the weighty tomb slips out into the museum room, held just within the painting's space by a cohesive rubbery glue that oozes over the foreground during its lava-like descent from French mountains down into the Louvre Museum, flowing without impediment onto the carpet of my New York apartment, three coincidental worlds in process of merging irreversibly into one. The words stretched out imprinted by the corrected man upon the rubber-covered tomb, read: 'YET IN ARCADIA HE GOES'. Turning herself inside out, surveying the museum's rubbery space, the Goddess approaches my gleaming, uncommunicative body sealed tight beneath the harsh spot-light, its sitting position, the Egyptian proportions of its seat, a seeming copy of the hieroglyph of Isis. Smiling at my expressionless state, she projects through the focused eyes of the cobra coiled at the centre of her head-dress, the completed phrase chiselled upon the black sarcophagus, adding by laser-light the last three words: 'YET IN ARCADIA HE GOES THE BLACK SHEEP'. The leather weight of the Death Goddess descends reclining on the rubber cushioning of my immobilised limbs, their animation suddenly suspended, becoming stiffened with rigor mortis.

Footnote: I became conscious just in time to see the beam of light receding into distant space. Reflecting on my experience, these events of last night, I believe with growing certainty that the black sheep still goes to Paradise, still inherits the Earth, albeit within a different universe or constellation, one that is subject to the divine law and religion of Heel!. The idyllic painting I have identified as being a perverse version of 'Les Bergers d'Arcadie' ['The Shepherds of Arcadia'] by the seventeenth-century French artist, Nicolas Poussin, who concealed coded within his imagery his worship of the Goddess. I understand from my reading of Heel! magazine that there exists a list of framed paintings and painted ceilings, through whose canvas and plaster, alternate worlds whose culture and religion are founded upon boot-worship, may be accessed by the initiated modern man. Bas-relief sculpture of the stiletto-heeled, booted, whip-wielding leather- or rubber-clad Goddess, through which the more physical man is forcibly removed at the moment of his orgasm, is the least subtle, most shocking [from the point of view of the restrained man] of the usual methods of exit and entry, this according to the letter received by me mentally from Heel! magazine's agony aunt, Madame de Morville, during my contemplation of a painting of her chateau near the Pyrenees by the same artist.

TWELVE

Venus in Furs

April 12th

Racking my fevered brain for a solution, confident that there was none, I had reached that peak of introspection when intellect and intuition, in whatever quantities then remained of these two qualities after a day of fruitless self-questioning and one-sided debate, fused together to form a single new faculty more penetrating by far and deeply intrusive into those more reticent portions of identity that are classified as sub-conscious. In case this journal of dreams should find a reader for whom the scarab-beetle is not the everpresent threat to life and increasingly rubber limb, who does not dress in a leather catsuit, in stiletto-heeled boots, or carry a whip, who refrains from following the law-abiding citizen back to his home to punish the uncommitted crime, then you will permit me to test your wits against my own that were subject to this sudden development into a higher faculty. A discovery has been made in Scotland, on an island in the Lake of Menteith, of a number of well-preserved pairs of female boots with 'kitten heels' and, as though 'ready to wriggle out of my grasp, being woken from hibernation like congregating snakes', an equal number of bull-whips. The island is not too distant and is easily overlooked from the island of Inchmahome to which the summer tourist travels by boat from the Port of Menteith. In fact there is a tradition dating back for centuries that not even the fisherman of rainbow and brown trout will set foot on the island of Inch Talla where the boots were found.

To simplify your task as investigator, we know that the heel when measured non-metrically, is reported to be one inch high on every occasion that the same measurement was taken. Two more pieces of information given out, both pertinent to your inquiry, are the Gaelic meaning of Inchmahome, being 'Isle of Rest', and the fact that the Lake of Menteith is the only lake in Scotland; it should, the reader will suppose, be named as a loch like for example the nearby Loch Katrine of which, strangely, Sir Walter Scott writes about the 'Lady of the Lake'. Also of interest is the mountain within easy walking distance of the Lake of Menteith, which is called alternatively, Ben Venue or Venus – Ben meaning of course mountain. The relevance to the solution to the problem of the identity of the wearer of the boots, if the sex is agreed to be that of a woman, of the above becomes clear when it is known that one of the Earls of Menteith is recorded to have released after his study of magical practices and formulae, etheric beings referred to normally as fairies, but for our more informed purposes, 'black devas', priestesses of the Goddess Venus. The Earl, presumably being himself aware of the true nature of his beautiful new companions, but lacking a sensible concern for his safety, he being of royal blood and his descendants being in possession of a prior claim to the throne of

Scotland, then sets them a task, that of fabricating a rope out of sand, their efforts supposedly resulting in the finger of land named Arnmach. Soon after, when he has been 'driven out of his mind', he agrees that this community of dark spirits with their liking for leather boots and whips, should be given a meeting-place, Coire nan Uruisgean, which is half way up the mountain to the west of the lake. In return, he retains the freedom to rule for an intervening period prior to the enthronement of the Goddess, and to continue as a sign of this seeming freedom, to call the Lake a lake rather than loch. And, so that the reader does not complain later that I have withheld information, I should add the strangest truth that the Earl and his heirs were required, by the time of the materializing of the Goddess' realm visibly in the physical world before the re-establishment of a matriarchal order, to have joined by marriage his royal blood with that of the black devas. A study of the line of descent of these true claimants to the Scottish throne reveals the name of Bogle, a word derogatory in its normal usage describing a goblin, or hobgoblin, but also a ghost or fairy. In time, according to what was then agreed by the Earl, his descendant who would consequently belong to both the human and deva evolutions, sharing an allegiance to the two worlds, his name being Malise, would be summoned by the Goddess, physically or subconsciously, to fulfil the rest of those conditions required by the agreement which was signed on Bogle Knowe, a hill near the lake which is associated today with supernatural activity and witchcraft.

No written record remains describing the physical meeting or etheric encounter, or verbal exchanges of the Earl and this witch Goddess who lived, according to that tradition handed down to us

orally, in Ben Venus, 'dwelling in a deep cavern within the mountain'. It seems that when the mountain is referred to as the
meeting-place of the black devas, it is called Ben Venue, but alternatively named Ben Venus, as the place of worship, by the visiting
pilgrim to the Goddess' subterranean temple. However, whether
by underground passage or a ubiquity of her divine consciousness
and therefore physique, whether etheric or otherwise, a Goddess,
named as well Venus and displaying the very same ultimate beauty
and possessing those same powers of enchantment and inclinaton
towards the imprisonment of men, was simultaneously reported
to be the subterranean inhabitant of a mountain in Germany called
Venusberg. The following written account may in truth be little
besides the duplicitous replication by some meticulous Teutonic
hand [being at the time short and empty of a similar legend] of the
period spent within Ben Venus by a Scotsman enslaved to the witch
Goddess.

Here she would lie in wait for men whom she would enchant and
keep imprisoned in the mountain forever. They would forget their
homes and loved ones – everything – while they served her and
were subject to her wiles. They no longer saw the sun or moon or
stars or the fresh green of the springing grass. Instead they lived in
a rose-coloured twilight filled with beautiful clouds, the heavy per-
fume of flowers and the scented leather of the laughing figures of
maidens – spirits of this mysterious underworld ruled by the witch
Venus. One night while this enchantress was watching and waiting
near the entrance to her grotto she saw a nobleman [the Earl]
chastely sealed within his suit of armour, alone and taking evident
pleasure in the condition in which he had been sent out into the

world of darkness by his absent lady, in the thrilling state of his penultimate confinement. He approached the witch's trap in the two confused minds of ancestral ruler and natural slave; she, who could read the hearts of men, knew who he was and whence he came, the future course of his life. Suddenly the rock door of a cavern swung aside before his gaze as if by magic, by his own dabbling or that of the inhabitant within. Beyond the dimly lighted entrance he saw a beautiful woman standing and stretching out her arms to him. Her dark figure was outlined by a halo, her skin polished by the rosy glow which came from within the cave. It was Venus who sought to lure him. Her terrible witch's eyes were hid behind a smiling face, and she was once again the fairest woman in all the world. Now she wove a spell while she beckoned him. 'Come', she said softly, 'I have seen your childish wonder and alone can bring you happiness. In my blessed land you will find all the pleasures and beauty for which you seek. Come!' Scarcely knowing what he did, the nobleman obeyed the enchantress and entered the portal. As he did so the heavy stone closed behind him and in that instant the memory of his previous life vanished like a dream. He had become according to his fate the kneeling subject of Venus. Taking him by the hand she led him far into the depth of her mysterious realm, and at every heeled step his wonder and delight increased. Here even the trees bore the ripe fruit of the spiked shoe and shining, unearthly boot. By her magic the waves of a smooth lake sang of strange love as they beat upon the shore. Here at last he thought he had found true beauty and happiness. And so he gladly served his queen as the years passed, experiencing them all as a single day. He had, as you know well, completely forgotten his

old life, and lived wholly in the present, entirely content with the
pleasures and suffering of his new life treating them as the same, as
though one was not better than or separable from the other.

But at last a change came over him. Something, he knew not
what, stirred within him and told him that he was a slave. He began to realise that he was under the power of a spell not his own,
and that he had given up many things for which he now dimly
longed. The watchful Venus saw his new mood even before he was
aware of it. She was full of anger at his appeal for freedom made in
spite of all her arts; but she hid her feelings behind a smile and
replied in soft tones, 'Whither would you fly? Are not all things
here in perfection? What more would you desire than your suffering at my hands?' She held out as an offering and flexed a whip in
readiness. 'I want only freedom', confessed her noble slave. 'What
is freedom? The earth you speak of has forgotten you. Here you
are immortal.' 'Still I would go away. I know not where. My Queen
give me leave to try another life for myself – something that will
meet this new-found longing within me. I will not be disloyal to
your memory. Indeed, I will sing your praise, and yours alone. But
give me leave to go!' 'Then depart' said Venus, her voice growing
cold with anger. 'Out of my sight, ungrateful mortal! But heed
well my condition for your freedom and release. Some day you
will return to me, and willingly, a descendant and offspring of your
self forgetful of this and other terms to our agreement which you
will sign, by which your kingdom, your line descended from Queen
Isis' Egypt, your inherited possessions, your people and self, the
very least subject, the last man, will belong to me and to my people, the fire devas, forever.' When the signing was quickly done

without his protest or due consideration of that distant future, she stamped down her heeled boot on the fixed ground and in a moment the scene was changed like the dissolving picture upon the projectionist's screen, back to the superficial world existing beyond her volcanic and erupting mountain.

As a constant and fitting reminder of whatever was agreed at that time between the mortal Earl and the witch Goddess [whether in front of him or behind his back] on behalf of her divine self as well as his future reincarnated self, three escallops, symbolic of the cyclic emergence of this Goddess into physical life, appear evenly spaced in a row on the Menteith shield, with below a leather feminine glove and implied bull-whip, and the words 'N'oubliez pas'. Another fact, surely irrelevant to any such investigation, might nevertheless be pointed out to the academic reader intent on a thorough study of the overthrow and fate of man: the trout flies used by the fishermen as bait on the neighbouring Loch Katrine, whose disappearance was announced simultaneously with the find of so many feminine boots on the island of Inch Talla, were named 'black spider, booby nymph, cat's whisker, ace of spades and damsel'. I will with luck finish this listing of facts and obscure relationships in a later journal entry. It is however, unfortunately the case that a woman from my dreams, wearing a black fur-coat, polished stiletto-heeled boots, carrying a whip coiled in her gloved right hand and with a Himalayan snow leopard on a lead in her left, appearing as if from out of some invisible hereditary shield, has followed me home and only the physical lock of my apartment door prevents our meeting.

THIRTEEN

The Parisian Cat-Woman

April 16th

Reading reports of a number of men in Antwerp, while viewing the painting by Alexandre Cabanel in the Koninklijk Museum titled *Cleopatra Testing Poison On Condemned Men*, collapsing in a heap upon the ground beneath the canvas, clutching their stomachs most vociferously until the point of death by her merciful boot-heels. In the Dorset countryside of south-west England where a third obelisk thieved greedily from her temple at Philae, had been re-erected in the gardens of the stately house, Kingston Lacy, the substituted Egyptian architecture is described as having stabilized for a period exceeding one hour before dematerializing. In addition I read revealed in this latest issue of Heel! how London's Kit Cat Club whose male membership had included several centuries ago, the architect John Vanbrugh and his patron, the Earl of Carlisle, is in fact dedicated to the organisation and purposes of Heel!, which would explain the recent moonlit visits paid to those grand houses designed for and by the members of that club, by the stiletto-booted whipwomen of Heel! demanding their immediate evacuation. The coating of external walls in black rubber and the dredging of the lakes [now filled with the same oozing liquid] dug out by the strangely named landscape gardener, Capability Brown, makes absolute sense of history's anticipation of today's change of political and physical climate, as does the hanging upon the internal walls stripped of their patriarchal art, of portraits of members of Heel! and their Council of Ten.

News of slave-ships arriving from Manaus in South America at the Cape of Good Hope in South Africa laden with their rubber cargo, and of the sealing of the island of Sicily beneath a coating of hardening black liquid that overflowed the volcano's crater, descending like lava upon the population of sleeping men and their rubber-clad, expectant wives. A large number of geneticists and white-coated male scientists have, together with their corporate and political paymasters, been dragged through those streets of London still free from the rising tidal water, before their drowning as belated offerings to appease the wrath of the approaching Goddess. In northern France, where the visions of materializing courtesans were once restricted to the garden of the Petit Trianon, the entire area of the Chateau de Versailles is transformed by the presence of countless, congregating members of Heel! dressed also, in equal numbers, in the same rubber costume worn by the riders of scarab-beetles. Reptilian creatures escaped from the fountains roam the inundated boulevards of Paris. Visitors to the Chateau of Anet which belongs to Diane de Poitiers, are described as having disappeared through a circle of light in the dome that 'appeared to move like the protruding eye of a chameleon in search of some constellation in the black night sky before transmitting the bodies of the female booted guide and the men gathered beneath the dome's circumference, into distant space'. A polished army of Amazonian women wearing black, curving breast-plates, while marching over the Pyrenean mountains by moonlight, was sighted last night by a Spanish shepherd tending his flock in the foot-hills below. Egypt is reported to have undergone a regeneration of architecture, even a wakening of long-preserved bodies, of thoroughly bound slaves and their mummified leather- or rubber-dressed mistresses; a partial explanation being no doubt the return to Karnak of the obelisk erected in Rome by Pope Sixtus V in 1588 [which had been vandalised by the addition of a crucifix to its apex], but not before that city had been subject to the random and spasmodic materializing of Egyptian buildings now occupied by newly recruited members of Heel!.

News flash from the Third World – by that I do not mean the world beyond or beside the other world of Heel! but that area of our material, Earthly world that has been victimised by the virile seed of the corporate giant, by the greed of the fat politician with his evil agenda, a President with a reptilian absence of human expression, fascinated by the electrocution of men. The vegetation, the genetically engineered crops and livestock, the environment itself, appears mangled and disfigured, the boundaries between different life-forms blurred and distorted as if by some molten volcanic rage of the Goddess, but instead by the hubris of mediocre men [without sense of the divine plan or nostalgia for its lost grandeur], listed name by name within the pages of this issue of Heel! magazine which has surely been distributed in London from where the first pictures of mob-rule, of mock and real executions, of rapid

justice meted out in the Banqueting Hall are being shown world-
wide. Medical scientists with blood on their hands are thrown from
the balconies of Cavendish Square by disfigured children grown
adult. No time, it seems, to be a scientist, good or bad. No doubt
it is precisely because the non-physical second, third, fourth and
fifth worlds are equally affected by the pulsing, co-dependent nature of existence, by Earthly man's true madness, that our planet is
being taken over, absorbed into that of the black devas.

A 'catwalking catwoman' wearing a leopard-skin furcoat and hat,
and black leather gloves, walking a snow leopard from the
Himalayan mountains, who has been spotted in Paris, was followed
by a simple man who gushed to reporters at their first inquiry that
in his [drunken] pursuit of this catwoman in her polished, stiletto-
heeled boots, as he had turned the corner into a dead-end street,
she had turned into [in some sort of shapeshifting performance]
the leopard, before disappearing with a leap into thin air. In a second location, in New York, below the skyscraping and polished
obelisks of a transformed Manhattan – its twin towers restored as
gigantic obelisks from their barbaric and tragic destruction – a solitary leopard is seen leaping over cars, from one side of the road to
the other, before itself disappearing, leaving behind only the sound
of stiletto heels clicking briefly on the sidewalk.

A colossal ziggurat-topped obelisk, coloured black and highly
polished despite its time, the millennia spent beneath the
Babylonian ground, has seemingly been pushed up into view, per-
haps triggering the subsequent and sudden emergence beside the
Euphrates river of the hanging gardens of the feared Queen
Semiramis, member of Heel!, member of the Council of Ten, and

representative of an avenging Goddess. The bitumen used in ancient times to coat and waterproof the huge stone walls of Babylon
during the flood – being manually smeared and brought to a shine
by her army of well-muscled but broken slaves – is replaced by
black rubber that oozes instead from crevices in the Mesopotamian
rock. St Mark's tower in Venice, beside the otherworldly version
of which the Council of Ten meet annually in the Doge's palace at
the time of the carnival, is reported to be suffering from an 'enclosing growth of black rubber' that emerged in the night from the
moonlit sea, scaling even during daylight, to the horror of this sinking city, this symbolic monument's full height, finally silencing the
age-old sound of its ringing bells. The wide screen of my television, my contact with the outside world during this interval of
terrible change, flickers to lifeless black . . .

FOURTEEN

The Servant's Contract

April 22nd

Last night I was witness to a strange pact, a piece of theatrical dream drama, the certainty of its physical re-enactment proved by the history of the sixteenth century in France, by the relationship between King Henry and his mistress, Diane de Poitiers, Duchess of Valentinois. To describe what took place, which characters took centre stage, briefly – since I sense that my time remaining in this your world is as the consequence limited – I found myself on the slope of a steep, man-made bank of the river Cher beside the Chateau of Chenonceau, gripping where mortar should be, looking over my shoulder at the silent water; yet there was only a stone bridge where today the nocturnal tourist crosses the river not in the open night air but within an enclosed gallery with windows to view [should she be sufficiently psychic as has been increasingly reported to be the case with the modern woman] the numerous ropes extending tautly down to the rippling or smooth, moonlit surface, at the submerged ends of which, attached to the masonry of this bridge that still exists – now tiled with black and white chequers beneath the tourist's stiletto-booted feet – are men who being originally also tourists have long since become during months spent in the isolation of the garden's ice-house [secured there with their polite consent, but more probably against their diminishing will], rubber-men better suited to the cooling river currents, being now more active by night beneath moonlight, their bodies hanging seemingly lifeless in the clear water during daylight.

I overheard a conversation between King Henry and his mistress, Diane de Poitiers, while he, reduced to wearing stockings so as not to interfere with the sound being transmitted through the heels of her polished boots [through the stone down the ropes into the re-shaped skulls of rubbermen], was following her in desperate pursuit up and down the full length of the bridge begging to be released from the agreement so rashly accepted that evening on bended knee under the influence both of drink and scented leather. The terms of the agreement, as I gradually came to understand them, being gleaned not from my surreptitious entrance within the chateau during their promenading absence and my inspection of a document with their signatures newly dried before a raging fire, but by my piece-meal reception, comparable no doubt to that of the attentive rubberman, of their echoing, often coded, close and distant exchanges, [he now whispering at her request, her forefinger within its leather-glove raised to her amused and disapproving, disciplining lips, she more strident yet concentrating all the while upon the messages sent below to her rubbermen by the routine clicking of her usually solitary boots . . .] were as follows.

Played out before me upon the smooth, moonlit water of the

River Cher, accompanying as though to aid me in my exact interpretation of the spoken word, or the clicked heel, I watched Diane
de Poitiers, re-entering as it were, the physical world but dressed
in the black of mourning, not however for her dead husband [as
would be commonly thought], but in anticipation of the imminent death of her devoted king and servant, Henry, who was,
though unaware of this future consciously beyond his forgotten
dream, to die in a joust wearing her colours, a final sign of the
everlasting bond between them. She would attend as representative of the huntress and Moon Goddess, Diana, appropriately
wearing an upturned, crescent moon as jewellery fixed dazzlingly
with a pin to the hair above her forehead. The lance of his oppo-
nent that would then after the climaxing of trumpets, pierce the
visor of his helmet, would reflect the mythological event of the
Goddess' killing of her mortal lover, the giant Orion, with an arrow fired from the beach upon which his body was later washed
up into her waiting arms. All this occurred in the reality of the
history of the sixteenth century taught ponderously by teachers,
repeated opportunistically by the lacklustre politician devoid of an
appreciation of the grandeur and theatre that delights the Moon
Goddess bored with mankind's secular and vulgar offerings.

In microcosmic parallel with the actions of the Goddess Diana
who had carried Orion's flagging body in her silver moon-chariot
and where the night was darkest placed him dead upon the river of
the sky, Eridanus, that he might be revived and transformed by
alchemy and the unnatural properties of the black viscous water,
her Earthly representative, the mistress, Diane de Poitiers, whose
consciousness bridges the divide between death and life, night and

day, then placed her medievally armoured servant, Henry, in the mist-enshrouded water of the River Cher – some black magical or wicca ritual being first performed by her rubber-clad ladies – where he continues to live, a stranger to himself, to his memory of her [beside the reminding vibration of her heels clicking on stone, their arrival and departure being as timely as any heavenly motion predicted by the astrologer], as her most enduring rubberman. The names and numbers of rubbermen and their swinging movement through the dark waters of rivers known to man and those invisible to his limited sight, are reported in the magazine of the organisation of Heel! – of which Diane de Poitiers is a member of the Council of Ten – and have been compared to the many oars of a trireme, except of course that unlike the slave chained or roped beneath the deck of a ship, the rubberman never moves beyond the transmitting sound of the stiletto-heeled boot, it being the last and vestigial link with his once human past.

Footnote: Inspired by Ovid's, *Metamorphoses*, the 'Story of Diana' tapestry that still hangs in the Chateau of Anet, another property of Diane de Poitiers, and which bears the ciphers of both her and Henri II, with its subject the death of Orion, was commissioned as a gift by the king prompted either by his own subconscious memory or the anticipatory demanding of his fully conscious mistress. Interlocking deltas [forming a star configuration], the monogram HD, as well as crescents are clearly evocative of the close ties that bind the king as eternal servant. The devotion of the king to his mistress is also evoked by the repeated use of their interlocking monograms in cartouches and on the base of a fountain on which Diane wraps her arm around the neck of a large royal stag. A sculpture of the Goddess with her bow, her arm again around the stag's neck, regarding the prey animal, is said to have been observed in animated dispute by a fleeing poacher. The original of this sculpture is confusingly housed within the Louvre Museum. It would seem likely, in relation to the above account, that had its author entered the Chateau of Chenonceau to inspect the agreement, he would have discovered that by the use of the interlocking monogram HD, Diane de Poitiers would as on other occasions, have signed on behalf of the king as well as herself, no choice being therefore given him in this matter of life or death. An account written by a male subscriber to Heel! magazine, reprinted in the leatherbound book, *Slaves of Isis*, by Madame de Morville, and titled 'The Bridge of Sighs', describes the slow process of transformation from vacationing tourist to rubberman in the subterranean and controlled environment of the ice-house.

FIFTEEN

Babushka Bay

I am eating May-fly as if the period of my hibernation in this New
York apartment depends for its healthy continuation upon such a
nourishing diet rather than the genetically modified food so far
consumed. My nails have become long like claws, my hands more
hairy than when last I looked, their skin now concealed as if in
adaptation to this prolonged and sustained siege by the scarab-
beetle. Perhaps if I were to offer a portion of this swarming seasonal
delicacy, then my own flesh, its brown hirsute skin, might be spared
from mastication between the formidable jaws revealed on each
occasion that the balcony window is tested for weakness, the attempt being made to prise apart its glass doors with skating, serrated
forelegs. Oblivious to the obvious sense of my rational thinking,
devouring by the pawful ever larger quantities of the briefly winged
fly so that I might more clearly observe the seaside environment
through their numberless eyes [the wave-like, ubiquitous consciousness of the entire swarm], I hear in complete terror the thunderous
sound of Mongolian horses sweeping irresistibly across the

Tsaganskaya steppe of Siberia. Responding to this all too familiar nightmare, on all fours, rejecting the hubris of my previous two-legged and human posture, I retreat as before to the cave's entrance in the primordially dense forest that skirts the edge of this glassy, inland sea [Lake Baikal, pronounced and written also as Lake Baigal, sacred sea of Siberia]. What century is this, distant past or nearish future? I watch the scene develop before my mind's eye, aided by each May-fly through the sight of which, skimming the melting ice, I search for the pale lavender marble and jade stones below, for signs of rubbery movement that each time accompanies the arrival of the mounted women in leather, the curving bodies of whom are further protected by skin that feels like mine.

The swarming May-flies are travelling fast, low beside the column of four-legged and chained men, all shackled and manacled, their necks joined in a crocodile, bodies whipped onwards along the Brown Bear Coast. Up and down the uncertain shore, the tormented men seized at dawn by this marauding horde of malicious and business-like women, are driven, cajoled at the point and heel of fabulous thigh-length boots with their accomplice in this slave-trading, the uncoiled and serpentine bull-whip. For long hours, only the nerpa [seal], their heads like black shiny balls rotating nervously upon the smooth sea, bobbing up and down in response to the perceived danger, the moment of sudden fear, appear and disappear, their black eyes seeming like empty sockets in a rubberized skull. Impatiently, these slaves-to-be are herded at dusk to Babushka Bay where one by one, the man being for this purpose disconnected from his companion, they are brought down to the darkening water's edge, forced forwards on their knees so that the head is baptised while the chosen buttock is branded by a single word, followed by the exclamation mark that to my bestial eye, aided by that of the confused and dying May-fly, signifies the property of the stiletto-booted organisation of Heel!. The head of this first man fights against the weight of the leather boot that pins him down submerged, rising from the viscous dark liquid water, blackened and no longer capable of inhaling the night air, before collapsing back down beneath the compassionate and acclimatising sole, a sizzling sound of cooling buttock-skin accompanying him in his descent beyond the May-fly's limited sight.

When all two hundred of these torch-lit, broken men had finally been branded, baptised, their skin then thoroughly rubberized, and a period of silence ensued during which the evaporation of sizzling surface rubber had dissipated, escaping into the night air, I watched as there appeared, looming above the lake, exposed to her booted thighs, a ghost-like, giant figure, similar in body size and terrible presence to that Colossus painted by Goya, but in contrast beautiful beyond a bear's powers of description. Moving slowly towards the shore, she rose at last to her full and divine height, sated by this exaggerated supply of new slaves, cracking her snaking and heaven-bound bull-whip above the heads of the temporarily subdued and awe-struck guards, in this fashion presumably acknowledging their good and valuable service. Synchronistically, a most powerful wind blows, seemingly generated by the action of the Goddess' whip which obscures her ghostly shape, returning this nocturnal scene to the verbal exchanges between unpaid slave-traders, who typically resolve to make up their losses by their hunting by full moonlight of sable and brown bear. I wake naked

═══════════

in a cold sweat in New York relieved to have again avoided capture and becoming the second skin of these Siberian whipwomen.

Footnote: The wind here referred to may have been the Barguzinski Wind, or Brave Man's Wind, which sweeps in violently from the Barguzin River Valley behind the Buryatian mountains on the eastern shore, or more vicious by far, the Sarma or Black Wind, from the west, which combines with the Barguzinski to raise up waves of 'astronomic height', so that 'when the Sarma comes, the heavens descend to Earth', writes expert, Semyon Lenin. It is the rumour, perhaps derived from a simplistic interpretation of the word 'Baigal', that this lake is some meeting- or mating-place for the dreaming bisexual woman, even of the lesbian and her late-night date. Also, it is believed by the academic that this word has the very same meaning as that of the Scottish 'bogle' which the dictionary defines as being 'spectre, fairy, scarecrow and bugbear'. The spectre that regularly appears above Lake Baigal and is clearly perceivable by the Siberian shaman with his functioning third eye, is described at the time of the full moon as shining with an inner, polishing light that is seen focused as a searching, predatory and cream-coloured beam that emerges through the forehead.

SIXTEEN

Kiss of the Spiderwoman

APRIL 30TH

Another night of wingless flight, this time prompted by my evening
reading, my studying and interpretation of esoteric texts from the
Taoist sacred books, my attraction to a passage written by the sage
Lieh-tzu stating that there exist, alive, immortalized on a Chinese
island, 'feeding upon the harsh wind and sipping dew, but eschew-
ing the five grains', goddesses that though they are surrounded by
mountain snow choose to dress in contrasting black, with coiled
whips. 'Their minds are like dark springs welling from deep gul-
lies, and they have the appearance of young girls'. Their skin, both
human and as well-tanned, in the case of the bull-leather of catsuit,
the stiletto-heeled boot or the narrow-waisted dress, is soft and
smooth and otherwise inviting. Possessing also a polished and rubber wardrobe, they are described as being 'strangers to fear and
love, commanding spirits and those mortal men that fall within
their remote and divine orbit', causing them to suffer in obedience
to each and every sort of their deplorable needs, bodily as fetish-
ists [requiring the attention of the servant's polishing-cloth],
psychologically as sadists.

The revered sage, King-sun Ch'ing, reminds his modern, god-dess-seeking reader who wishes in profoundest error to extend such devious and painful pleasures indefinitely, that although coming face to face with these booted and immortal ladies is so improb-able an experience that years must elapse in the fulfillment of this self-defeating quest, the possession of a discarded boot, with or without its pair, when treated together or alone as if still occupied and owned by the invisible goddess, will suffice as the elixir. Such a stiletto-heeled boot was I believe left on the balcony of my tower-block apartment by a scarab-beetle intending to draw me out into the New York night then to grab at my pyjama-ed torso with its serrated forelegs. Waiting until the coast was clear – by which I obviously mean that for some reasonable time no scarab-beetle was seen within the vicinity of my apartment – and reaching discreetly over the dividing, waist-high wall to my neighbour's dinner-table upon which the careless and mistaken creature had left this female boot, I retreated deep into my bedroom where I was to clean and polish the surface, first wiping away the powdery Oriental snow.

Having admired the curves of its/her perfect shape, inhaling her aromatic scent to the point of intoxication and sudden exhaustion, I awakened from a light sleep, finding myself flying [as I had in-tended at the moment when I was about to descend into and through my dreams] above the Eastern Sea off the coast of the Shantung peninsula, through air that was sufficiently more dense than what is natural, to suspend both physically and mentally the animation of numbers, of countless men dotted about the night sky, above and below me, on all sides. Beyond this interruption to my night vision, this multitude of seemingly disconnected and rub-berized men, in the distance at ground level, I saw the snow-covered peaks of P'eng Lai Shan, etheric island of the immortal Goddess, existing also within the realm of dreams and more recently reported as being materialized physically: 'From towering peaks [of the Shantung peninsula], one gazes upon an island-dotted sea of tremendous depth and often so rough that gigantic waves rear up like mountains before hurling themselves upon the rocky coast. In a strong wind when the waves crash upon the cliffs, their spray resembles a profusion of silvery pearls being scattered upon the rocks by heavenly nymphs. At other times, mists sweeping in from the sea take the form of strange goddesses . . . There are moments when the moonlit peaks of a mountainous island are seen rising from a sea of silver mist that veils from sight the ocean; and it is recorded that in winter when the weather is propitious, a mortal man worthy of stupendous gifts from the three Fates, can see in the far distance the peaks of P'eng Lai Shan, island of the smooth-skinned immortal ladies. He is permitted a fleeting glimpse of the rubbery other world wherein the polished girl plays with the lust of man, and with his mortal life'. The moon shone down through this tangled web of dreaming men that were each joined by a glistening rubber thread to his nearest neighbour, so that the male population of New York, feasting its eyes and fat stomach drunkenly upon a diet of fetishistic ingredients, was during the night transported to China, to the world of these previously extraterrestrial ladies, then hung out to dry in the oriental sky caught in the web of a cosmic spider, a shapeshifting Goddess with a human face. My mental alertness, my painstaking flight amongst the now wriggling men – whose twisted fate was being sealed by the full moon's creamy light that was melting each rubber fibre wound about their tortured, metamorphosing forms into a seamless and polished cocoon – brought me safely and normally conscious down to the surface of an alien Earth which was itself sealed beneath the snow by a coating of smooth black rubber upon which stood as though grown out of this living raw material, with the incorporated stiletto-heeled shoes and boots as organic fruits, the oriental architecture of the feminine and immortalized inhabitants with their endless supply of imperishable spidermen.

Such new and reconstructed men as these cocoons soon will become, it is revealed by close study of the texts of Lieh-tzu and Kung-sun Ch'ing, are indeed fortunate, being favoured by the three Fates, becoming in time immortal according to the variety and purpose of their new physiques [whether they are to act as polishing-servants using their multiple legs as tireless aids or to be the mass-producing creators of new boots], when they are fed through what remains of their human mouth-parts with the ripened fruit of the stiletto tree, *Palmetto Stiletto*, which contains all those rubbery elements into which the interior of the cocoon has metamorphosed beneath full moonlight, the process being initiated by the touching kiss of the Spiderwoman: 'Whatever mortal man inhales that strange atmosphere, becoming enamoured with the pleasing nature of her human face [that of the Spider Goddess], digesting as well her ripened fruit, he takes into his very blood the thrilling of the elemental spirits and they change the senses within him, his notions of space and time, re-shaping each contour of his masculine body and mind, so that he can see and be perceived only as the stiletto tree [its organic and feminine architecture] can see and be perceived'.

SEVENTEEN

The French Kennels

MAY 4TH

I should admit that were this personal journal to fall into human hands and not the chewing jaws of the intruding beetle and the question is put to my perhaps vacantly expressive torso still tied to this chair reluctant finally to be hoisted by those serrated insectoid legs into the New York sky, I have for the reason of decency deleted the journal entry for May 3rd, so vile and rude were the experiences of the previous night as to be best not preserved even in this scribbled, possibly illegible form. There is a level of propriety below which I am as unwilling to venture as into the darkness of this beetle-filled void beyond the glass boundary of my apartment's balcony. Suffice it to say, in case the reader is clad neither in leather or rubber, wears sensible shoes commensurate with the mild climate and possesses at least a residue of human sentiment and concern, an academic interest in the completed record of these awkward and resticting times, the deleted account was of time spent on the four – nearly as many legs as those attached to the exoskeletal beetle – legs of the canine best friend, whose allegiance is switched from man, his previous identity, the species to which he has so contentedly and for so long belonged as a proud upstanding member, to that of the heeled, booted woman who carries a whip coiled fashionably in the street, reserved domestically as this new human dog's nocturnal treat.

To be on all fours, behaving as a dog, which was I confess my true position yet shared by so many muzzled and despairing men in the courtyard of the Louvre Museum, permits when one is still a reasoning creature not expected to volunteer one's contributions to the conversation of this new café society, [to comment upon fashions when one is blinkered at first light and so familiar only with the chosen shoe or polished stiletto boot], a reflection upon this bizarre and most unwelcome change of personal circumstances, with a perception and insight exceptional for the intellectual, academic man lacking the instinctive and associative processes of thought common to the walked or tethered dog. Though it is common knowledge that a rubbery growth which hardens slowly beneath the creamy rays of full moonlight, has taken hold of, smoothing out the rough surfaces of the city of Paris, there has been a minimum of speculation, human or canine, to my knowledge when acting as a two-legged and bound recluse or sniffing street-dog, as to the future state of the society for which this new environment has been so painstakingly produced by the alchemy of moonlight and black rubber both infused by some divinity who is or are deliberately favouring the feminine and the sensual in place of the old brute order.

Why is the first area of Paris to be occupied by this otherwordly, in origin and beauty and dress, community of wriggling and catwalking women, located within easy reach of the museum, its subterranean environment accessed by a gleaming rubber pyramid materialized at the centre of the courtyard – having the same appearance, proportions as that pyramid in some way inserted within my own head which despite the determined pulling out of my hair and much besides through nasal tubes, remains the night-time vehicle of my removal to distant places and alien, less temperate climes? Behind the silenced bark, where beard and dog's hair meet and merge, turned from one into the other, back and forth, until stabilised by collar, lead and boot, the Louvre, its true meaning, its Latin translation, occurs to me during the relinquishing of my earlier receding and school-time memories to be the word, *Lupara*, which means 'Kennels', the ancient status of this popular museum. Is this new world order of Heel!, [its membership of polished women and physical organisation on planet Earth] then to be founded in such a bizarre and anachronistic fashion upon out-of-date translations as much as the mistaken identities of modern and muzzled men? Or is the dog's proximity to the once fertile gardens of the Tuileries the justification for such vile, rude and unnatural behaviour in the courtyard of the Louvre?

EIGHTEEN

Lady of the Lake

MAY 10TH

'Tannhauser', the word whispered darkly in my ear woke me with eyelids closed, with mosquito bites searing the leathery skin of my dreaming face, fearful of the repellent and decadent nature of the perverted household into which my consciousness had been inserted together with my no doubt well-bound and tethered body. What filthy brothel, what sort of diseased and sickening bordello, which city, Paris, Berlin, or Rome, would I discover to be the location of this unwanted dream? I was forced by reason of the movement of my legs, the wriggling of my torso, to surface, to engage myself in the lewd and lascivious atmosphere that would be the certain environment of what is more honestly categorised as worst nightmare. Yet, though my arms were not free, both remaining invisible throughout the duration of this experience, being strapped, wrapped by the rubber fabric tightly behind my back, I was privileged within the new community in which I now found myself in enjoying the freedom to walk upright and after a short time inquisitively, curious as to why the feminine inhabitants seemed frozen in and by time and not by the equipment of the bondage room [though the provision of rope and chain appeared at first inspection to be locally supplied, no doubt freely available, in the most genuine of dungeons that I was certain lurked unseen below ground level in this French chateau in Burgundy].

'Tanlay', the second word heard, whispered anonymously by my unseen female companion, [who was I believed responsible for this plucking of my dreaming body from some pleasant and more polite domestic scene into her nocturnal world], whose invisible and stiletto-heeled shoes or polished boots sparked on the medieval stone, crossing the reflective, dark moonlit water of the Chateau of Tanlay's moat. Appearing however to my bewildered, focusing sight, as though in dire need of moisture to lubricate the rubber of their clothes [suddenly in danger of perishing from a ray or shaft of alien and summery starlight brought with me from my world], tall women in an elegant line standing, bending, kneeling, three or more deep, along the edge of the moat, seemed to be about to launch themselves, diving desperately into the healing water. And yet, even while appearing in this manner to clamber - a word which utterly denies the true native elegance of this stunning sight - over one another to be first to immerse their black and gleaming skin, by some power [being the unknown and natural possession of the mere human male] I had frozen these several hundred women [possibly more, for beyond where the moon light reached, a black indistinct mass of rubbery flesh continued into the distance] in mid-step or -flight. What a minor restriction the stiffening bondage applied to my upright upper body seemed relative to the helpless plight of these perishing or perished women to whose aid I hurried breathlessly in the thin air, so that I might dislodge them one by one, pushing them into the water by the weight and extension of my free and functioning legs.

On my approach to the first in line, judging from a few steps away that I was mistaken in my quick analysis of their predicament, I realised all too late that it was not any excess of sunlight or masculine power that had caused their condition but the extremity of their beauty preventing them from leaving the sight of their reflections below in the moat. For how many of our centuries had this paralysed state been endured by these expressionless leather- or rubber-clad polished ladies? Was I some knight dreamed up by them in their feminine need for release, a distraction brought on by my whispering and severely booted guide whose naked outline was at last clearly visible to my twisting torso, and whose appearance I recognised in a sudden flash of lucidity to be that of Diane de Poitiers, a painting of whom representing by her beauty and nudity, Venus, hangs staring outwards at the disconcerted visitor, in the Earthly version of Tanlay? Appearing rejuvenated, newly returned to this duplicating environment of lighter air and greater beauty, she attracted to her body as if by the modest thought, the furcoat, boots and bull-whip customary in her other world. Whether she wore leather or rubber or some more polite and less cruel clothing beneath the black fur, there was not time for me then to imagine, for I was by the jagged, vicious pulling of a neck-chain, the brutal kicking of her pointed boots, the coiling of her whip around my torso, myself selected as hairless and human guinea-pig to test the viscosity of the moat, to prove its healing power and safe action upon my newly completed but armless, rubber skin.

'Die Tannhauser!', she pushed my exposed chest – my kneeling, battered and whipped body which leant backwards over the edge of the moat – with her booted stiletto-heeled foot so that the glassy, impenetrable surface was shattered with a splash. I, like some operatic hero, had freed the ice-maiden from the imprisoning, cold night, from her fixed and narcissistic condition. Slowly descending into the cooling water that healed and closed above me, facing upwards, my own glassy and vacant stare the substitute for the newly animated faces that plunged after me, after their own reflections, into the deepening invisibility . . . at length when my bubbling descent had turned finally back to a reanimated and lively ascent, so that I could swim without arms like a tadpole, if not for that reason reach out to touch the moving boot, the Goddess as she walked on water as though stiffened with ice, I rose beneath a moonlit lake as smooth as Tanlay's moat, as slave, not hero, nor romantic knight or prince, but as perpetual slave to Venus, to her emerging army of polished devas. A sinking feeling, the gradual eclipsing of my dreaming mind and body, brought me round again, the securing of my physical torso to the apartment seat being surely the reason for this perhaps brief respite from that otherworld of cruel ladies and their reflections.

NINETEEN

Cape of Good Hope

MAY 16TH

A giant scarab-beetle hovered outside my apartment during the night, eyeing me hungrily through the expanse of reinforced glass, testing its surface for accumulated weakness before disappearing back into the darkness. The only illumination in New York is provided by the strengthening shafts of alien starlight. Were the cables of electricity severed by the serrated forelegs and crunching mouth-parts of hordes of unseen scarab-beetles? Unable to sleep for fear of lucid-seeming dreams, of finally losing myself completely to that other world. In order to remain awake, I am therefore – perhaps as a last written journal entry – setting out below the research notes made some weeks ago relating to the Opera House or *Teatro Amazonas* in Manaus, in case they might prove useful to any future reader who survives these catastrophic, apocalyptic times, a free man [to help preserve him in that most improbable condition].

The interior space is described as being shaped like a harp. Alternatively, the volume of the auditorium is described by another authority as being enclosed by the shape of a flexed bow, that of the feminine inhabitants of this jungle region which comprises the Brazilian state of Amazonas. To me, it appeared to be womb-shaped, the red carpet being the symbol of blood. The Eiffel Tower reproduced on the dome with the central chandelier surrounded by a circle seemed obviously to reflect both the Parisian vortex to which the location of the opera house is linked, but as well the kundalini charge of sexual energy required to dematerialize and then to instantaneously transport the individual man who descends by the French chandelier with its inevitably Italian crystal, to within range of the flailing, taunting array of bull-whips which mimick the tails of sperm. The overt reason for the chandelier's downward mobility – that of the cleaning of its bronze and crystal and renewal of its lights – strikes the informed investigator with one flying foot planted infirmly in the camp of the esotericist, a third eye lost in the detail of *trompe l'oeil*, as superficial, deliberately disingenuous.

The *Teatro*'s stage curtain, painted in Paris by the Brazilian artist, Crispim do Amaral, who is, I discover, but not to my surprise, commissioned by the familiar organisation of Heel!, depicts supposedly and only, the local Indian water goddess, Yara or Iara, which may otherwise be spelt by the decoding change of 'a' to 's', and 'r' to 'i', keeping the four-letter length, as Isis, who is of course recognised in Egypt in the guise of the serpent Nile goddess. Also, if we are still in the process of extracting multiple meanings, Iara appears reclining naked in the escallop shell in which the goddess Venus is typically portrayed at her birth into the mundane world of mortal men. And if we recall the Venetian contribution to this jungle building, it is perhaps also a reflection of the meeting between Poseidon [bearing his cornucopian gift] and the reclining [enrobed] Venice as shown in the painting by Tiepolo and as well by Tintoretto. Proceeding with this line of inquiry, I discovered that the vertical height of the stage, including the dome into which the curtain is stiffly raised, is a colossal 75 metres, added to which and to my fascination and extreme terror, I noted that in the original architectural specification, there is the strictest requirement that the frontal part of the stage should be able to be lowered by at least three metres below its regular level, this to accommodate the height of the diva's heels!

A further requirement, the installation of which I myself witnessed during my descent from the dome, was the placement of the heads of twenty-two [do not ask me to explain this number if we should meet as slaves in the Republic of Venetia] tragically masked men fixed on marble columns, appropriate to this amazon's theatre. Nor is it surprising, but macabre and morbid on first reading, this fabulous building is the subject of male fantasy, of phantasmagoric tales of fine ladies wielding bull-whips in their leather opera-gloves, their black furs worn cruelly over eighteenth-century evening dresses or the most tight-fitting of undergarments made from wild, pure rubber latex or from the tanned, trimmed and sewn skins of jungle hides. Such theatrical scenes have of course been reported more recently and widely as being 'commonplace' in the gardens and in the Hall of Mirrors of the Palace of Versailles. The *Palacio da Justica* near to the *Teatro Amazonas* is reputedly modelled on the architecture and practices of Versailles.

Outside, I can confirm that though the grassed gardens and statues were in fact imported from England, the dressed stones are made from a local blend of rubber, clay and sand, an effective and black composition intended to dampen the noise of hoof and foot, and of the lady's chariot. The city of Manaus is raised on the shore of the Negro river, a few miles from the meeting of her dark waters with the more lightly coloured Solimeos river [which has nevertheless been reported to have been blackened under the former's influence in recent months], forming the Amazon river by their confluence then flowing more than a thousand miles to the Atlantic Ocean. Given the increasing viscosity, the rubbery properties of this liquid water, the figure provided in Heel! magazine [my subscription to which I now greatly regret] that the Amazon river produces a litre of water for every person on the planet, every twenty seconds, will surely appal the reader the internal organs of whom have not yet succumbed to their conversion from water to rubber. It occurs to me as I write down this information, that the titling of the stage-curtain painting, 'Meeting of the Waters', and the fact of the Rio Negro's current predominance of both colour and texture in the greater Amazon, might indicate the changing darker mood of the Goddess, her waters polluted and fouled by the materialism of man.

I must draw attention to a seemingly innocuous, innocent-sounding project devised by Heel! for their overthrow of decent traditional civilisation, which is described in their recruitment literature and magazine as the setting up of an 'Ecopark', indeed a 'Monkey Forest', where researchers [of quite a different character from myself] work in rehabilitating monkeys that were captive and are to be returned to their 'natural environment', performing their natural activity of tapping the wild rubber tree for latex which is to be then supplied of course free to the opera-going membership of

Heel!, and for transport by slave-ships bound for the Cape of Good Hope in South Africa. I should make one final point illustrative of the degree of subterfuge and strange humour possessed individually by the female members, collectively by the organisation of Heel!: the pink dolphin native to the Amazon is named *Boto Rosa*, an anagram of Botas Oro, concealing from the honest man-in-the-street, were he still to exist, a reference to the French 'Order of the Golden Boot', created medievally and most cruelly by Eleanor of Aquitaine. No doubt the changed colour from pink to black of this dolphin, and the facade of the *Teatro Amazonas* both indicate the imminence of the global catastrophe intended for man by the black devas and their Goddess.

TWENTY

The Trampoline

MAY 17TH

I am woken abruptly by the staccato sound of stiletto heels upon marble. We are grouped beneath the *trompe l'oeil* ceiling of a Venetian palazzo. The guide dressed in a polished leather catsuit worn by the membership of Heel! is pointing to the black figures of heavenly women that peer down upon our male bound flesh longingly. Smeared blood stains on plaster seem to the imagination to float like clouds about the soon stirring beauties whom we are being instructed, despite this evidence to the contrary, possess no human blood within their painted veins. So what liquid courses through their enlivened, divine, soon flying forms I seek to ask through masked and sealed lips? The instructing whip, still coiled about its leather glove, points at my completely rubberized physique, at its roped torso with arms withdrawn tightly behind my back, then directs my dislocated limbs upon a trampoline squarely placed beneath the ethereal, booted scene. I begin to bounce to the rhythm of the guide's bull-whip cracking in the thinning air above me, between me and the responsive ceiling, upon the trampoline's black elastic sheen higher and higher past the darkening, rubbery skin of the pilastered walls, to where the scarab-beetle lurks behind the bloodied cloud, its rider familiar, motionless, frozen, about to pounce. Higher still I fly from the rubber trampoline up through the distant sky until grabbed at last between the serrated forelegs. Held out from beneath the beetle's undercarriage, being now approved by the stiletto-booted rider, finally I'm captured within the dark atmosphere of the otherworldly, moonlit, eternal night . . .

Appendix

The following ten-step method of entry into the Republic of Venetia was given out by the Council of Ten in a recent television bulletin intended for the whip-wielding, stiletto-booted Mistress impatient to experience the otherworldly pleasures so frequently described in the pages of Heel! magazine. The rest of the text of this brief broadcast – addressed not only to the rubber-clad Mistress but as well to the kneeling slave – is printed in its entirety as chapter fifty-six of the book titled *Slaves of Isis*, written by the agony aunt of that magazine, Madame de Morville.

1. First discover for your slave and yourself an empty beach with sand sloping gradually down to the sea where he should be positioned kneeling looking out to the horizon. The sea, like your slave, should be placid and the day sunny with uninterrupted views, or alternatively, lit by a full moon.

2. The slave is instructed to focus his mind entirely upon your rubber-suited form as you move backwards and forwards across the sand in front of him, his attention being primarily and naturally directed by the monotonic sound of your voice, by the force of the repetition of your command, to the shape and gleam of your boots.

3. The purpose of this exercise, practised often in the domestic

environment before the attempt is made, is to still your slave's mind, to shut off his thinking processes, until only the single thought remains, his undistracted admiration of your boots. The consequence of this moment of suspended animation extended into the future, is that the calm sea extending to the horizon becomes frozen to his perception.

4. You must enter this moment with him and experience a new continuity of time within this moment. As soon as you detect in his dreamy, unblinking eyes that the moment has arrived when his world has stopped, and you have confirmed his state by testing with the heels of your boots the viscous, then hardening surface of the moonlit sea, then he should be encouraged in his dumb state to follow your lead onto the water.

5. Whether he is on two legs or four, whether he is saddled by your weight or walking beside you collared at the end of a leash, proceed confidently out to sea, towards the horizon upon which after a certain amount of this new time has elapsed will be revealed distant architecture, the topmost portion of buildings, which may at first appear almost familiar, as if taken from your dreams or once visited as a tourist out of season.

6. As you progress to the point where the outline of similarly dressed ladies may be perceived dimly, if not as yet clearly, and you are perhaps nervous, being so far from the perceived safety of the sandy beach left far behind, and fearing that the fixed concentration of your slave may be about to waver so that you will sink into the sea far beyond your depths . . . remain confident that you are approaching the outer limits of the Republic of Venetia, where your future and that of your slave, lie.

7. Your saddled slave, perhaps blinkered and squinting at the spurred boots both pressed against his seemingly sunburnt flesh, will hardly have noticed the sudden transformation beneath his tiring feet from sea that is frozen in time to that which is frozen in ice which signals in your apprehensive mind your successful transfer, together with your slave, from the no-time condition to that of the painfully slow time of the moonlit Republic of Venetia from which we transmit these messages of encouragement and guidance.

8. Do not look back. You will have learnt how to visit our world in full waking consciousness, using the mind and body of your slave as your unwitting vehicle of transport. What was previously accessible to the Mistress and slave only in dreams will become like the tourist's favourite destination to which she returns time and again in spite of her husband's unheeded protests; though in this new circumstance such a contradictory mood is of course no longer available to his stunned and perpetually manipulated mind.

9. The return journey is identically made by the combined operation of the Mistress' intent and the stopping of the slave's thoughts brought to the sole attention of her passing and polished boots that like the clock's pendulum in the leather-gloved hand of his female hypnotist, still and silence his internal world.

10. One final point, before the Mistresses are invited to join us at our table, is to remember on the occasion of each of your visits to the Republic of Venetia to present your slave for initial inspection as to the required levels of docility and boot etiquette, to the Venetian Tourist Police.

Select Bibliography

Morville, Madame de, *La Dominatrice* [Stiletto Books, 2000, ISBN 0–9525463–7–X].

Morville, Madame de, *Slaves of Isis* [Stiletto Books, 2000, ISBN 0–9525463–6–1].

Morville, Madame de, *Slaves of Isis: Volume Three* [Stiletto Books, 2000, ISBN 0–9525463–8–8].

Morville, Madame de, *The Chateau* [Stiletto Books, 2001, ISBN 0–9525463–3–7].

Morville, Madame de, *Temple of Isis* [Stiletto Books, 2001, ISBN 0–9525463–2-9].

Morville, Madame de, *Slaves of Isis: Volume Four* [Stiletto Books, 2001, ISBN 0–9525463–9–6].

Morville, Madame de, *The Priestess* [Stiletto Books, 2002, ISBN 1-903908-06-X].

Heel! Magazine, published by Stiletto Books for the Paris Offices of Heel!. [Internet website: www.HeelMagazine.com]

Graham, Robert, *Night Vision: The Powers of Darkness* [Matrix, 2000, ISBN 0–9525463–4–5].

Final Request

The following pages have been left blank so that the male reader may be encouraged to begin recording his own experiences on a nightly basis which in time may provide a complete account of his mental and bodily conversion and removal to the world of Heel!, to the Republic of Venetia. We, as is our purpose as publishers, would hope to have your journal returned to us from that other world by the Venetian Tourist Police [into whose leather-gloved hands your writings will inevitably fall] for study and subsequent printing. May we express our gratitude in advance for your pioneering work in the field of expansive consciousness and for permitting us insight into the future that lies ahead for the mass of ignorant men when the time comes for the final merging of the two worlds and the domination of the surviving rubbermen by the new world order of Heel!.

STILETTO BOOKS

❧ HEEL! ❧

⊷§ HEEL! §⊶